One Minus One

One Minus One

by Ruth Doan MacDougall

Introduction by Nancy Pearl

Text copyright © 1971 Ruth Doan MacDougall

Printed in the United States of America.

Published by AmazonEncore
P.O. Box 400818
Las Vegas, NV 89140

ISBN-13: 9781612183220
ISBN-10: 1612183220

Introduction

I FIRST discovered Ruth Doan MacDougall in 1965 when I was a junior English major at the University of Michigan. At the time (and for many years before and after, although no longer) *Redbook* magazine would include a complete novel in the back pages of each issue, and it was there that I came across MacDougall's first novel, *The Lilting House.* The pages of these novels in *Redbook* were always both darker in color and heavier than the other pages of the magazine. Perhaps for that reason, and because *Redbook* was explicitly a magazine for adult women, and I didn't quite feel like a woman yet (these were the years when "don't trust anyone over thirty" was the prevailing ethic in my sociopolitical circle, and none of us was in any hurry to grow up), reading those novels (and I always read them) felt to me daringly illicit.

I adored *The Lilting House* when I read it, but didn't pay particular attention to the author's name, so I never connected it with three other novels by MacDougall that I greatly enjoyed over the next eight or ten years: *The Cost of Living, One Minus One,* and *The Cheerleader.* After reading those, I was always on the lookout for any new novels by her. I especially hoped, as I'm sure all of us who read the story of Henrietta "Snowy" Snow in *The Cheerleader* did, for a sequel to that particular book. Although that was not to be until *Snowy* was published in 1993, in the meantime MacDougall wrote a number of other novels that I enjoyed, including *Wife and Mother* and *Aunt Pleasantine.* But, to close the circle of this reminiscence, around 1990, while I was working at the Tulsa City-County Library as the head of the Collection Development Department, I found an "ex-library" copy of *The Lilting House* at the library book sale.

Remembering how much I had enjoyed it, I purchased the copy and then discovered, to my amazement, that it was written by one of my now favorite writers, Ruth Doan MacDougall! I was so thrilled to connect *The Lilting House* with some of my current favorites that I went on a reference search for her address (no small feat in those days) and wrote her a fan letter. (I hadn't written to a writer since I was twelve or thirteen years old and sent a poem of mine—inspired by his novel *Street Rod*—to Henry Gregor Felsen.)

So when I was thinking about what novels I'd like to include in the Book Lust Rediscoveries series, it was almost a forgone conclusion that at least one of them had to be by Ruth Doan MacDougall. After much mulling, I decided to begin with *One Minus One* (the first section of which, I just discovered, also appeared in *Redbook*, although I hadn't read it there).

When I talk to librarians (and librarians-to-be, in the Reader's Advisory classes that I teach at the University of Washington), I like to say that there are four main doorways through which one can enter (or be drawn into) a work of fiction: story, character, setting, and language. My "dominant doorway," so to speak, tends to be character (second is language). So it's not surprising that what most draws me to MacDougall's novels are the characters she creates. For me (and I know that this isn't the case for all or even most readers), plot is far less important. In fact, the plot of the novels I'm most taken with almost always seems to grow out of the nature of its characters: it's who they are that seems to determine what happens in the story. These are novels in which the characters are three-dimensional, can't be summed up in a sentence or two, and are much more than a type or an archetype. They have a body and blood, bones, and brains.

Such characters aren't simply slotted into the story, like cogs in a machine, to serve the process of the story's unfolding. Examples of this might include the wizard who the story's protagonist depends on for guidance and strategic aid (e.g., Gandalf, in J. R. R. Tolkien's *Lord of the Rings* trilogy); the noble cowboy/

gunfighter who rides into town, helps the overmatched family man in his battle with the bad guys, and then rides out again (e.g., Shane, in Jack Schaefer's novel of the same name); or the brilliant detective who is characterized by his numerous eccentricities (e.g., Rex Stout's Nero Wolfe). Now, as much as I've loved reading these books, their biggest doorway is story. And although I'm a huge fan of these three authors, it's not the depth of the characters that draws me into them the way it does with other novels. In character-driven novels, I can easily imagine them walking down the street, sitting next to them in a coffee shop, or standing behind them in line at the grocery store. They're not necessarily like anyone I know (or, for that matter, not necessarily like me), but they do seem familiar in a reassuring way.

Unlike a lot of readers of character-driven fiction whom I've talked to, I don't necessarily have to like these people (or approve of their decisions or support their choices), but I do have to be able to understand why they do what they do. In Tim O'Brien's *In the Lake of the Woods*, for example, I don't have a whole lot of sympathy for John Wade, the main character, but I believe I know exactly why he did what he did. (And, by the way, for curious readers, yes, I do have *some* sympathy for him.) Similarly, I defy any reader to admire the way the eponymous main character in Elizabeth Strout's Pulitzer Prize–winning collection of linked short stories *Olive Kitteridge* behaves, but I totally get the reasons why she acts out her toxic unhappiness. (Incidentally, I was one of the judges for the Pulitzers the year Strout won, and it was certainly one of my top three books of the year.)

Another indication that a novel's characters are three-dimensional is that upon finishing the book I can't help but wonder what might have happened to them next. I'm left not just with a sense of regret that an engrossing and enjoyable reading experience has come to an end (and now I'll have to find something else to read) as I might be with, say, a good, plot-driven thriller, but with a sense that I've been hanging out with a group of interesting people that I've grown to know well, and I'll miss them.

Our choice for Seattle Public Library's very first "If All of Seattle Read the Same Book" was Russell Banks' *The Sweet Hereafter*, which is divided into four parts, each of which is narrated by a different character. Always, when Banks spoke to audiences in Seattle, one of the first questions he was asked (and it was my question, too, the first time I read the novel) was "What happened to Billy Ansel [one of four main characters] after the book ended?" Now that's the sign of a writer who has created a character that's become part of a reader's life. I can't imagine a higher compliment to give a writer.

And that's exactly what Ruth Doan MacDougall does in each of her novels. The characters are recognizable, familiar (sometimes uncomfortably so), and alive in my mind. I want to know more about them. I want to know how their lives turn out after the end of the book. Especially Emily, the narrator and central figure in *One Minus One*. Since 1971, when I first read *One Minus One*, I've thought about Emily a lot. Without giving too much of the plot away, I'll simply say that MacDougall sets up a dilemma for this divorced woman who's making her way through her fourth decade: How do you go on with your life when everything that you counted on (love, a husband, a way of life) has been willfully annihilated by the very person you most trusted? Do you listen to your heart or your head?

I'm sure that some readers will become impatient with Emily's behavior; they'll feel that she's wallowing in her sorrow, that she should put the past behind her, move on. There were times during rereadings of *One Minus One* that I felt this way— I've wanted to (gently) shake Emily and tell her to stop behaving like a child, to grow up and pay attention to the opportunities the future holds. Other times, though, I understand completely why her heart can't let go of a love that's now doing her no good at all, and I can't bring myself to fault her for it. And, really, in the end, who's to say which offers the best guide to how to live your life, your heart or your head?

I hope you enjoy *One Minus One* as much as I did.

Nancy Pearl

TO PENELOPE DOAN

CONTENTS

One Minus One

THE MORNING MAN

I said to the cocktail waitress, "Is there any way to get to Hull without going around that damn traffic circle?"

"Well, miss, there's the old way through Portsmouth."

I peered at my map in the gloom. "I know, Route One-A, but is it marked or does it let you end up lost in the middle of downtown?"

"Sorry, I guess I never noticed," she said, and picked up my empty glass she'd replaced with a new gin and tonic, and moved briskly off.

In the bar, it seemed that outdoors didn't exist, although I knew that outdoors it was afternoon, and hot, and the sun sizzled on the blue ocean. Labor Day.

I had wanted a long drink when I'd left the beach, but I didn't want one alone in my attic apartment, and as I drove down the road I saw that a big old camp had been made into a restaurant. SEASIDE RESTAURANT, its sign said, though it was not on the seaside of the road; COCKTAIL LOUNGE, it said. The place looked clumsily friendly. I'd hesitated, for this would be another ordeal, like driving distances and going to the beach alone. I never in my life had gone into a restaurant alone, much less a bar. You have got to do it, I told myself, there are hundreds of things you have got to learn to do now and not all of them are mechanical things like driving a car and sharpening knives and adjusting a TV picture. My hands had begun to sweat as I turned and drove toward the restaurant.

Inside, in the pine booths with red-checked tablecloths, many people were eating whatever meal people eat mid-afternoon in restaurants, and the smell of fried seafood was hot and thick. Waitresses galloped. Everyone, it seemed, looked up at me as I came in, a lone woman wearing an old cotton skirt and blouse, and I nearly fled, but that would have been even more embarrassing. A little sign said LOBSTER BUOY LOUNGE, and I stepped through the doorway into a darkness so sudden I had to wait moments until I could see the people on the red-cushioned benches behind small tables, the people on the high stools at the bar. Where did a woman alone sit, at a table or at the bar? The women here were no help; they were all with men. But the bar might be a vaguely disreputable choice (memories of peroxide blondes in gangster movies), so I slid behind a table and sat down on the bench and ordered my drink. Feeling very brave, sipping the drink rather too fast, I studied the map I'd brought in to have something to do.

Now, with my second drink, I was brave enough to look around. There were indeed a great many lobster buoys hanging from the ceiling, and clamshells and starfish were arranged in the mesh of the fishnets on the walls. The jukebox was singing "Galveston."

The man at the next table said, "Route One-A is marked pretty clearly, and anyway, all you have to do is follow the signs for the Spaulding Turnpike."

Oh, my God, I thought. This was something else I'd never had to cope with, unless you counted guys saying "Hi there, baby" to you in the street, or guys in cars honking their horns and yelling at you out the window. And then there was that time in Boston when I was walking alone to Jordan Marsh while David, who hated shopping, was exploring Beacon Hill, and a guy grabbed one of my breasts. Not that there's much to grab, but he did, and twisted, let go, and kept on walking. Despite my panic, my first worry was that somebody had seen, yet no one had.

I ignored this man and looked at the map again.

He said, "That traffic circle is a nightmare today, isn't it?"

And my feelings about the traffic circle were so intense I forgot to maintain silence and said, "I honestly didn't think I'd make it around it alive." It had been much worse than I remembered. At all four entrances cars from Maine and Massachusetts and

New Hampshire were backed up as far as I could see, we New Hampshire cars, we natives, waiting at the western entrance to try to creep through to get to our bit of coast. The circle was a spinning madhouse.

He said, "They're building an overpass, that'll siphon off some of the traffic."

"It used to be awful, but not so bad as now. I couldn't believe it."

"Then you're from around here?" he said.

"No," I said abruptly, trying to repair the situation.

But he said, "I'm Warren Goodwin, I work at WHNH." Which was Hull's radio station; I'd seen a billboard that told me to tune in. He said, "What do you do?"

Self-conscious about calling myself a writer, I'd always called myself a housewife. I remembered what I was now. "I'm an English teacher."

"Where?"

So he was the kind who kept asking question after question. I disliked the type, yet admired it because I wished that when I wanted to know something personal I too could ask right out, but I didn't dare because it wasn't polite and instead I waited for the information to be volunteered; sometimes it never was, so I never knew.

"In Millbridge," I said.

"Been there long?"

"This will be my first year."

"Where'd you teach before?"

"No place."

I could see that now in the dimness he was trying to judge my age. Once in a while when I was with David I'd had to show my driver's license to get a drink, and although I didn't believe I really looked under twenty-one, apparently I didn't look so old as I was, either. At least not in the dark of a bar. Did I now, alone? Was I beginning to look no age, the way most women did between twenty-five and thirty-five?

He said, "This your first year out of school?"

"Good God, no," I said, but pleased. I was thirty. I began to feel somewhat friendlier. I glanced at him. He seemed tall, and he had long sideburns.

He said, "I thought you said you didn't live around here. You don't live in Millbridge?"

"It's probably the most hideous town in New Hampshire, I can't imagine who does. Though I expect I'll find out."

"Then you must live in Hull."

"Well. Yes."

"So do I. How about another drink?"

"No, thank you," I said, yet the reason was I'd just remembered I had to drive home. How easy, how lovely, it'd be to be a passenger once more.

He said, "What's your name?"

It hadn't been so hard to learn to say my maiden name again; it was when signing my name I forgot and wrote "Emily B. Lewis." I said, "Emily Bean," and picked up my pocketbook.

"Well, Miss Emily Bean, since I don't use the traffic circle on weekends or holidays, I'll be going back through Portsmouth, so why don't you follow me and we'll see you don't get lost."

"Oh," I said. Then, "Thank you." I looked at the map. "After Portsmouth, it's got to be the Spaulding Turnpike, has it? There's no old road?"

"The turnpike's the only way nowadays. Hell of a situation, isn't it?"

"It sure is," I said, and, remembering the check, reached for it just as he took it off my table. "Hey—"

But he was at the bar, paying the bartender. Below fishnet bunting, bottles glowed, opal and emerald.

"Thank you," I said.

We went out through the restaurant. I'd come in alone; now there was a man walking behind me. Had I got picked up?

Outdoors, the shock of light and heat was like a blow. We squinted at each other.

"You won't lose me," he said. "I'm the bus."

It was an old blue Volkswagen bus with bright decals of flowers stuck all over it, and WHNH was painted on one door.

I said, "This is mine," and he opened the door of the middle-aged Falcon for me and I got in. But I didn't really think of it as mine; it still seemed David's, and I hadn't wanted it, although at last I took it because this was most sensible since Ann Turner had a car herself. Sensible swap. And now I didn't have to move the seat up as I always used to the one time a week I did the grocery shopping and the laundry; now it was always in the right position for me.

"By tomorrow," he said, looking at the cars streaming along the narrow coastal road, "they'll all be gone. The place'll be deserted."

"Thank heavens," I said. I buckled my seat belt.

We joined the stream, and I followed the bus past the beach. It was a state beach now, and a wealth of cars was parked in the parking area, and you had to pay. I'd paid, and on the sand littered with the empty Fresca cans and potato chip bags people had left, the Wonder Bread bags once packed with sandwiches, the beer cans and greasy french fry containers and crumpled cigarette packs spilling out of trash cans overturned by seagulls, I had found space for my beach towel between a family of parents, grandparents, children, picnic hampers and coolers, all under a beach umbrella, and a boy and girl who slept holding hands. I was always very serious about my tan, but this summer, what with the job hunting and the apartment hunting, I'd had only a few chances to lie in the sun in my mother's backyard. The beach was terribly crowded. A radio was playing, and voices around me seemed even closer than they were. "Billy, don't throw sand." "Have you seen Joyce? She looks like a hippopotamus on vacation, and I told her so." "Billy, you want to go home?" "Somebody bring the camera." "You get wet and I'll kill you." "See my seaweed!" "Billy, do it again and we'll go home." I had dozed, alone at a beach for the first time in my life.

We drove past the cabin colony where David and I had stayed during our honeymoon. I'd been able to avoid seeing my grandparents' camp farther down the coast, but I hadn't been able to avoid this. There were more cabins now, so I couldn't tell which one was ours, and a pond had been built since, on which sailed ducks and seagulls and swans. Cars were pulling off the road to watch them. I followed the bus past pleasantly awful big old camps, past the picture windows of horrid little new ones. There was the smell of the salt marsh, and then the ocean could no longer be seen.

The emptiness came back as I drove. Or, rather, it had been there all along, but now I was aware of it again. A great hollowness inside me.

I drove across a short suspension bridge, the grid jarring me in just the same way the grid of the bridge entering Concord had when I was a kid; the bridge, the special whine of the tires, the constant tug underneath, a scary massage, had been something to look forward to on trips. That bridge was replaced by a modern one now.

Then there were houses, and a cemetery whose many graves had a fine view of the harbor, and through the crowded streets of the old seacoast town I followed the be-blossomed bus, past glimpses of narrower streets and proud old houses.

Then we jounced along the detour around the overpass construction, drove past houses and gas stations out to the turnpike, and still the bus was always ahead of me, leading me over the new bridge beside the old bridge, each one-way now, across the bay to the Hull exit. Our directional lights flicked on.

At the stoplight on Main Street I flicked my directionals again but Warren didn't, and when the light changed to green he went on ahead while I turned; the bus gave a Volkswagen beep, and I honked my horn. So that was that.

• • •

The house was tall and white, deep in the old residential part of town, and its street had more trees left than any other street. Green leafy quietness.

I parked in front of the house, because there was no parking space allotted in the garage for the attic apartment, and collected my pocketbook, towel, and beach bag from the passenger seat and got out. I looked up and down the green street at the big comfortable houses. Then I looked way up at the window in the eaves, my living room window.

It was a long climb. Already I thought twice before I took down the garbage. On the first floor lived an elderly couple, Mr. and Mrs. Crabtree; when I came in yesterday from buying milk she had opened her hallway door and invited me in. Mr. Crabtree was nearly blind, and so was their fat wheezing beagle. Their house, Mrs. Crabtree told me, had got too much for them a few years ago, and they had moved to this nice apartment. With, evidently, every stick of their furniture. She showed me pictures of children and grandchildren and of the house, a white farmhouse.

My landlady, Mrs. Dupuis, lived on the second floor. So did Mr. Dupuis, I supposed, although I hadn't seen him there yet, just in his car as he drove off to work. It seemed an odd apartment to have chosen to live in, sandwiched between the two other apartments, but perhaps they preferred to put up with it and make the extra money the first-floor apartment must bring. Mrs. Dupuis herself went off to work at some office every morning in a rattletrap Chevrolet.

After the second-floor landing, the stairway narrowed and grew steeper and darker. My door was a makeshift accordion one which pleated back as I opened it. I was in the kitchen. I put the towel and bag and pocketbook down on the gleaming pink Formica tabletop and wandered through the low-ceilinged rooms. Everything had been spotlessly cleaned by Mrs. Dupuis before I moved in last week, the linoleum shining, crisp doilies on the backs of the old overstuffed chairs, a new lampshade in its cellophane wrapper that I dared not remove, the starched and ironed bureau scarf, and the satiny turquoise bedspread. The smell of wax and detergents was still fresh. Nothing belonged to me here, except my clothes, the sheets and blankets and the china and silverware and TV set, my typewriter and my five-string banjo.

The apartment had been made out of only half the attic. The other half had been left as it was, for storage, and although I had forced myself to explore it and discovered nothing more sinister than old chairs, a foot-treadle sewing machine, some trunks, and a great deal of dust, I still didn't like the idea of its being there behind that door in my kitchen.

The rooms were stifling. I turned on the air conditioner in the kitchen window; it made a horrible racket. In the refrigerator freezer was the pound of ground round I had divided into quarter-pound foil-wrapped pillows, and I took one out to defrost for supper. It looked ridiculously small.

After I had stripped off my skirt and blouse and faded bikini, and rinsed out the bikini in the washbasin, I couldn't think of anything else to do. I could take a bath, but sweating I would go into it and sweating I would emerge, nothing accomplished except washing off the dried salt which I rather liked on my skin. I put on my bathrobe and examined the clothes in the hot closet under the slanting roof. Staying home writing all those years, I had accumulated mostly slacks and sweaters for autumn and winter, so I'd had to buy some new things to go to work in, a little skirt and jacket, a frilly blouse, a turtleneck jersey, a brief dress, a pair of square-toed shoes, and two pairs of panty hose—my version of a basic wardrobe I'd no doubt recalled from some fashion magazine or even, oh, God, my home economics course back in junior high. Soon I'd buy more, when I started getting my pay. Here the new clothes hung, and the old skirts and dresses from school days at Brompton State College were all shortened and mended, everything very clean and ready for tomorrow. The terror of the first day at school. I felt as if I ought to have bought a pencil box.

I went back to the living room. I would read, and then I'd have a drink and watch the news on TV, and then there'd be supper, and then there was the evening to get through. I sat down in the chair near the window and picked up my murder mystery. The doily on the little table beside me was plastic. Evenings, the evenings. I'd read of people doing this, but I never thought I would: in the evenings, alone, I was afraid to look in the mirror because I'd find I had no face.

The telephone on the plastic doily rang. It'd be my mother, in Saundersborough.

"Hello?"

"Hello."

I'm no good at identifying voices on the phone, not even David's, and for one wild searing moment I thought it was David. Sweat drenched my hands. "Hello?"

"Hello."

It wasn't, because David knew my difficulty and by now would've said who he was. So this must be either Warren Goodwin or an obscene phone call (another first!) or maybe both. In my anguish I myself was rude. "I *hate* people who don't immediately give their names," I said fiercely. Then I thought, oh, good Christ, what if it's the principal or somebody?

"Hey, I'm sorry, this is Warren Goodwin."

"My number isn't in the phone book yet."

"I called information, simple as that. Would you like to go out and have some dinner tonight?"

"Thank you, but I've got to start work tomorrow, there's a teachers' meeting."

"What time?"

"Nine o'clock," I said.

He said, "That's the middle of the afternoon for me, I have to be at work by six."

"Six in the morning? My God."

"I'm the Morning Man," he said, and he seemed to say it with pride.

"Oh," I said.

"So we wouldn't stay out too late. What do you think?"

I was thinking of the little pillow of hamburg. "Well," I said.

"Would you like to go back down to the Seaside or somewhere else on the ocean?"

"Oh, no, that drive's too nerve-racking to do twice in one day."

He said, "Is there any place in particular you like around here?"

"I don't know any place, I've just been here a week."

"That's about what I figured. Okay then, what kind of place do you like in general?"

"Well," I said again, and paused. There were only the opinions developed with David. "I don't like restaurants where you get great huge meals, I mean I like the meals but you eat too much and feel awful and it's always sort of disappointing, it's not special, it's not much different from Sunday dinner when you were a kid. It's simply got parsley added."

"Then what's special?"

"Something you can't make so well at home. Is there a Chinese restaurant?"

"Nope. There're some along the coast."

"Haven't I seen some pizza joints around town?"

"Only two serve beer. Or do you like Coke with pizza?"

"Egad."

"Then let's go to one that has beer," he said. "I think the Pizza Hut's pizza is better than the Den's, okay?"

"That's fine."

"Unless you'd like one of Hull's other specialties. The Burger Chef? Stan's Submarine Sandwiches? Colonel Sanders' Kentucky Fried Chicken? The Dunkin' Donut? Lum's steamed hot dogs with sauerkraut? A&W Root Beer? A Dairy Queen?"

"I'd like a pizza, please," I said decisively.

"Where do you live?"

"Fourteen Brewster Street. My car's out front. My name's under the doorbell."

"See you at five thirty. We'll go have a drink first."

"Okay. Thank you."

I hung up and wiped the wet receiver with the sleeve of my bathrobe.

It all seemed very peculiar, in the bathtub, washing off the salt, shaving my legs; I felt that I was back in high school getting ready for a date with David. When I got out of the tub I rubbed the mirror clear of steam and looked at my face. My hair, light brown, had been cut extremely short ever since I was in the eighth grade. So I could wash it now, and it'd be dry by five thirty.

• • •

Waiting, I had badly wanted a cigarette for the first time in weeks. As Warren helped me up into the bus, I said, "Would you happen to have a cigarette?"

"I stopped a couple of years ago."

"Oh," I said. Saved. "So did we. I. Then I started again and stopped again. Good Lord, this is just like a real bus, isn't it? I mean, there's nothing in front of you."

"I think your seat belt's down here, I'll get it."

We hauled the belt up through the crack in the seat, and he helped shorten it for me. The bus was too old to have come with seat belts installed, so he must have bought them. And he actually used his, as David did.

He said, "I'm afraid Hull doesn't have much to offer in the way of drinking places."

He had to drive like a real bus driver, too. Sitting very high, we chugged down the street. I glanced behind me into the back and saw a sliding pile of LP records, a towel, some empty beer cans, and a pair of sneakers.

I said, "Wherever you want to go is fine."

"Let's try the Hampshire."

It wasn't far. The hot summer evening, the quiet old streets. Then some gas stations, and we drove down into the motel parking lot. Beyond was the turnpike, busy with cars.

"Everybody's going home," he said.

How strange to walk into a motel lobby with somebody else. The cocktail lounge was dark and air-conditioned, icy cold. People were secret at little candlelit tables. We sat down in a booth and were secret ourselves.

"What would you like?" he asked.

I wasn't driving. "A martini, please."

"Two martinis," he said to the waitress. "Very dry."

The seats here were red, like at the Seaside, but the decor, I realized as my eyes adjusted, was decidedly different. Yet what on earth was it? Big fake beams, coats of arms on the walls, crossed swords above the bar. Baronial? Through the suave strains of Muzak, the television told us how many people had by now been killed this holiday weekend.

He said, "Did you have a hard time finding an apartment?"

"It's a furnished one, there were only a few decent ones to choose from, and none at all in Millbridge. It's the best I looked at."

"It's in the good section of town. Mine's a real dump, I keep meaning to hunt for another one but I never get around to it, so I've been there six years."

The martinis, as I expected, were not dry.

He said, "Where did you grow up?"

"Saundersborough."

"I'm from here, Hull."

I said, "When we used to play you in football and basketball, we used to call you Hell. Got a night game in Hell, we'd say."

"What class were you, when did you graduate?"

"Fifty-seven."

"I bet you were a cheerleader."

"Does it show?"

"I was class of fifty-nine," he said, "so I wouldn't've been playing yet when you were cheering, but I'd've been watching."

And we were together, long ago, in gymnasiums.

I said, "My sister cheered, too; she was class of fifty-nine." He was Susan's age, twenty-eight. My baby sister. I remembered, irrelevantly, that my father had been seven years younger than my mother. I said, "Your colors are red and white."

"Yours are—don't tell me, I've got it—they're purple and gold."

I ate my olive. "You can't imagine how hard it was to buy gold underpants to go with our uniforms," I said, and stopped. Then I thought, oh, so what. "The stores in Saundersborough had to stock them specially."

He said, "The cheerleader I used to go out with wore *two* pairs of underpants. Red ones."

"We wore two pairs, too. It's a matter of being discreet during cartwheels."

We began to laugh, and on the television the news program showed highways of speeding cars just like our turnpike outside.

"You don't have any rings on," he said. "You don't even have a mark where a ring might have been."

"We got married in school and there wasn't any money for such nonsense. Anyway, my hands are too ugly," I said, displaying them, the writer's bump on my right middle finger, the nails of my left hand filed very short, the banjo calluses on my fingertips, and the many little white scars where warts had been removed. "It used to be even worse, when my writer's bump was yellow with nicotine."

"You were married."

"Yes. I play the banjo, that's why these nails are so short, for fretting."

He touched the writer's bump briefly.

I said, "I learned to type in high school but it never completely went away."

The waitress materialized and asked, "Would you like another?"

He looked at me. I said, "Whatever you think."

"Sure," he said. When she left, he said, "You must've written a lot."

"I guess I did."

"Do you still?"

"I'll have to see if there's time, now I'm working." Stupid answer; if I wanted to enough, I would make time.

"What do you write?"

"Novels. Stories."

"I'll be damned. Are any published?"

"No." I drank some new martini, and, desperate to change the subject, I very nearly asked a direct question. "I don't have a radio, so I haven't listened to the Hull station. I remember the morning program my mother always used to listen to, the guy kept calling the listeners 'gummy eyes,' which wasn't particularly pleasant when one was trying to eat one's Cheerios."

"You get a radio, and I'll play 'Green Eyes' for you," he said, and I was more startled than flattered that he'd noticed, since I wasn't used to anyone's noticing, and anyway it was only because my jersey and eye makeup were green that my eyes were green tonight instead of no color. He said, answering what I didn't quite ask, "That's about all I do, play records and try to keep things lively enough so I'm waking people up, not putting them back to sleep. And I read the local news."

"That itself must be mighty lively."

"You bet it is. 'At five P.M. last night a car driven by Roger St. Jean failed to negotiate a turn on High Street and struck a utility pole; no one was injured. Vandals last night broke into Pete's Grocery, robbing the till of forty-six dollars and fifty-three cents. Stay tuned for the marine weather forecast after this message from Kimball's Camera Store.'"

"Hey, I'll have to buy a radio so I can get the no-school announcements when it snows. I suppose you do Millbridge."

"We do everywhere. 'There will be no school today at the Winnie-the-Pooh Nursery School.'"

Even these wet martinis seemed to have begun to numb the hollowness; I could pretend it was simply my hunger for supper. All at once I felt very chatty. "What a crazy place to find myself, Hull and Millbridge, the last place in the world I ever thought I'd end up, I've always hated it down here. Except for the ocean. But I had to pick up some credits, you're supposed to get six credits every five years if you teach and I'd never got any, and I figured I might as well get them at the university so I might as well work near it, I'm absolutely no good at driving anywhere, I expect to be killed every minute."

"What are you taking, English?"

"No, I guess I'll take some stupid education course." And here it was, the opinion I'd formed completely by myself. "It just suddenly seems quite ridiculous to take lit courses, whenever I get looking at them in the catalog I want to go throw up. Education courses are even more ridiculous, in a way, and I certainly got my fill of them as well as lit at Brompton, but I think I could stand it better because I don't give a damn about education."

"That's the spirit," he said.

I heard myself laughing. Candles trembled in the dark red room. What a crazy place for me to be.

"Come on," he said, "let's go have our pizza."

"Okay."

Outdoors, it was still the long pale evening saved by the daylight saving. He helped me up into the bus. I was being taken care of again.

• • •

I ate the last of my share of the pizza and said, "I wish these places would choose some other color, what is this thing everybody's got about red?"

"I guess it's supposed to be warm or something."

And, despite the air conditioning, it was, warm with the smell of oregano and oil. When we went outdoors, the smell stayed with us, into the bus, but as we drove off down the street of gas stations and discount department stores and bowling alleys and supermarkets, neon signs shouting at us, it faded away into the smell of exhaust fumes. I wished it hadn't.

Warren said, "This is called the Miracle Mile."

"What's the miracle?"

"I don't know. Money, maybe."

"God, I like pizza. Thank you, that was awfully good." If only, I thought, it hadn't been such a red plastic place, if only it had been a wonderfully filthy beer joint like the one we used to go to in Brompton, Garafano's, which looked like a long wooden houseboat moored on a stark field, and where Mrs. Garafano, thin and freckled, stood behind the bar and talked across her baby set upon it, and students drank dimies and ate meatball sandwiches, and the people from the farms sat in booths whose tables were crowded with thick plates of steak rinds and scraps of french fries growing skins of grease. Now and then their children would clamber down from the seats and run the length of the room and back again; from the jukebox Connie Francis whined songs; and Mr. Garafano in person, a square dark man wearing a T-shirt, with a dish towel tucked into the waistband of his trousers, would come out of the kitchen to bring you your pizza.

Warren was saying, "I've got some Canadian Club at home, do you suppose that would mix?"

I prefer scotch, I thought before I thought, oh, Jesus, *now* what do I do, when I knew of course I could simply say no. I looked at the Timex watch I'd bought this summer; I'd never particularly needed a watch these past years. Eight thirty. I must have been thinking of the apartment, the mirror, the terror of tomorrow as I said, "Canadian Club would be lovely."

He turned at a gas station whose signs called out that its automatic car wash was only ninety-nine cents (without wax), and we drove past decaying duplex houses, an old factory, a grimy meat store—COST PLUS 10 PERCENT!—up a hill into the backyard of a big shabby house layered with asphalt shingles, gray in the twilight.

"Home sweet home," Warren said. He opened the door. "When I couldn't stand it any longer I used to go over and stay at my folks' for a while, but they moved to Florida last year. Sarasota. I guess I've really got to start hunting for another place."

I lived in an attic; he, I realized as I stepped into the kitchen, lived in a cellar. But it was nice and cool. He turned on the light and I saw the gray cement walls, the ceiling so low it made him seem even taller, a small cellar window uncurtained, the empty can of sloppy joe sauce and a plastic bag half full of hamburger buns on the counter, the candle stuck in a Chianti bottle on the little wooden table. A pair of blue sweatpants was thrown over a chair.

But no matter what he said about the place, he seemed to grow more easy here, like anyone coming home. He opened a cupboard and took out a fifth of Canadian Club, although the tumblers he next took down were decorated with labels of other kinds of booze—a Cutty Sark and a Beefeater's.

"Is water okay?" he said. "Or ginger ale, I think I've got some ginger ale."

"What?" I said. I had just noticed political stickers stuck on the brown tile floor as if marking a trail; HUMPHREY AND MUSKIE, they said, NIXON AND AGNEW, PETERSON FOR GOVERNOR, KING FOR SENATOR, and disappeared into the next room. "Oh, that's fine, water's fine."

"Those things are left over from last year," he said, opening the yellowed refrigerator. "The girl I was going with, she wasn't old enough to vote but she'd worked for McCarthy and she wanted to have a party and stay up all night and watch the returns come in on TV and get drunk because everything was so rotten. And we had this big party, but I don't know how late everyone else stayed; I went to bed." Ice clunked. "Let's go sit down."

We followed the red-white-and-blue trail into the living room which was very small and dark and crowded with a sagging sofa and armchairs, a lobster trap for a coffee table, and an elaborate stereo. There were more candles in more wine bottles. He lit two, and I saw that one wall displayed a poster of Nixon looking tricky; it asked, WOULD YOU LET THIS MAN SELL YOU A USED CAR?

Warren put a record on the stereo, fussing over it. "Heathkit," he said. "Built it myself."

"Really?" I said, and sat down cautiously on the sofa. Springs could be felt but were not painful. The room reminded me of apartments people had when we were in school.

"It'd've cost about three hundred bucks," he said, "if I'd bought its equivalent. I made it for two hundred. Hey, what's the matter, are you crying?"

"No, of course not," I said, and I truly wasn't, I was only on the brink, and I was always on the brink these days. "It's a beautiful stereo."

Peggy Lee sang about a spinning wheel.

"Scared about school?" he said.

I said, "All I've ever done is practice teaching, and that was nine years ago. I hated it then and I'll hate it now."

He sat down beside me and balanced his Cutty Sark glass on the slats of the lobster trap. "How come you didn't do something else, then, go to Boston and get a job in an office or something?"

"I don't know, I never thought of that," I said, surprised at the idea. "I just thought of teaching. I sort of automatically took the education course at Brompton, my mother's a teacher, an elementary school teacher, and she went back to work when my father died, and I figured an education would be like insurance, I knew I'd never want to teach, but it seemed sensible, something definite I could fall back on if I had to. So now I've fallen."

"Tell you what," he said. "Do you like to run?"

"Run?"

"What time do you suppose you'll get out of the meeting? I'll give you a call and we can go over to the track at the park and run, you won't believe how great it'll make you feel."

"Run?"

"I run a mile every afternoon. You'll have to take it easy, for a start, maybe just one lap and see how you feel. How *do* you feel?" he said, and kissed me. The sofa cushions began to slide slowly forward, but just as I thought we were about to land on the floor he braced us back; he was apparently much practiced in coping with this sofa.

Illicit was how I felt. Did I expect David to come storming in on us, me with my jersey now rucked up, and this stranger? Stop thinking of David. I touched Warren and was actually astonished that he was the same as David; I'd known only theoretically that other men were. I told myself, well, you decided to keep on taking the Pill so you wouldn't get ghastly cramps as you always did before, free of cramps you are, and also free for this, revenge on David, but David is free of you and he doesn't care. Then we were standing, and the cushions slid down like a dark-brown avalanche.

What the hell, I thought. We went toward the bedroom. The only bachelor bedrooms I'd ever seen were pictures in *Playboy* magazine; this certainly didn't look like them, except perhaps for the candlelight shadows. No bedspread, just a blanket and sheets on the bed. A beer can and a box of oyster crackers on the bedside table. A television on the old bureau. And Warren on me, tentative but urgent, our clothes slipping off, and when he kissed my breasts the shock was like that time I got grabbed, and, suddenly resenting his violation of God knows what, certainly not my virginity, I almost pushed him away, and then a mechanical excitement began, and then, even though everything about him was wrong, he was too tall, his hair was dark, not fair, he smelled of a different aftershave, a different deodorant, mechanical excitement bloomed into delightful excitement and I thought, he likes me, I can't be nothing if he likes me, and I hugged him to me. Afterward, we laughed at a silly program on TV and ate stale oyster crackers.

• • •

It already had become a habit to spend my free period and my lunch period in the teachers' room, but it didn't occur to me why this seemed so natural until now, as I was scraping the last of my cottage cheese out of my thermos jar. David, I thought, it's because David had the teachers' room habit and he'd talk more about teachers' room conversations than what happened in his classroom. Until the last year, when he didn't talk about school at all.

Kaykay Harrison crumpled up the aluminum foil which had wrapped her half sandwich and dropped it in the wastebasket. She said, "I wasn't as hungry before I started as I am now, and I was starving then." She opened her pocketbook and took out a pack of Salems. "Want one?"

"Thanks." It had also, since that first jittery day at school, become a habit to bum a cigarette once in a while. I wished Cliff Parker, the head of the English Department, would come in; he smoked Pall Malls.

Kaykay was about twenty-four, taught social studies, wore an engagement ring, and was dark-haired and pretty. "Just look at them," she said, "and almost every one of them at least ten pounds overweight."

I inhaled menthol, and, dizzy, sipped my machine-brewed coffee and looked at the people eating sandwiches and at the people with trays of the hot lunch which today was a slice of ham covered with raisins in a sauce that resembled phlegm, accompanied by mashed potatoes and pickled beets and a square of applesauce cake. The men were discussing the pros and cons of buying snowmobiles this coming winter; the women, except for a lanky practice teacher named Valerie Something, were talking about a student they suspected was pregnant. The small beige room stank of cigarette smoke.

David's teachers' room in Thornhill High School was the boiler room. There were two wooden benches, and a chicken-wire fence around the boiler, and the janitors washed the garbage cans cozily nearby. Every year out of the eight we lived in Thornhill David would petition for a proper teachers' room, and every year the administration decided, of course, that all the rooms were needed for classes. Maybe, at last, he grew fond of it, because it must have been mostly where he talked with, grew friendly with, and fell in love with Ann Turner. Romance in the boiler room.

Kaykay said, "You know Grace Fifield, she teaches business, we share an apartment and we swap making lunches, she'll make them one week and then I will. When it's my turn, I practically sit right down on the kitchen floor and bawl, I have to make her a *whole* sandwich and pack some pickles and some Fritos Corn Chips, for God's sake, and some cookies for dessert. She's one of those people who can eat anything and never gain, and I had to end up rooming with her. I tell her she ought to've warned me, she ought to wear a sign. Watching TV at night, she'll sit and eat a bowl of *ice cream*."

The door opened and Cliff Parker came in. "Ice cream?" he said to Kaykay.

"Sorry, I was just talking about it, I haven't got any."

He went to the coffee machine and then sat down near us in an overstuffed chair whose plastic upholstery was ripped. "I hope you weren't talking lightly, ice cream is a very important thing." Out of his sport jacket pocket he produced a package of Nabs. This was his lunch. Sometimes they were cheese crackers and peanut butter, and sometimes they were malted milk crackers and peanut butter. He said, "Do you ever go to the UNH Dairy Bar? They've got the best ice cream around. But it's all so good it's a hell of a decision to choose which kind. I've been known to vacillate for fifteen minutes in front of the flavors sign."

His hair was thick and curly, and so was his beard, and both were nearly equally a tangle of gray and brown. He couldn't be more than thirty-five; was gray still premature at that age?

Kaykay said, "Chocolate walnut, that's the only flavor in the whole world. At least, if my memory serves me; it's been so long I've forgotten what it tastes like."

"Try what I do," Cliff said. "Go over and have a cone for supper. For your whole supper." I had assumed he was married; this sounded as if he was single. And watching his weight, how funny. But Warren went jogging; yet that was for the exercise.

Cliff said, "Sometimes I sin, however. I have a sundae."

"Oh, stop it!" Kaykay wailed. Then she asked, "What kind?"

"That's another terrible decision, but it's usually hot fudge."

Kaykay said, "What kind of ice cream in it? I always felt that chocolate walnut ought to be best, but actually vanilla is."

He said, "Coffee also should be considered."

"My fiancé, Bob, that's what he says his favorite flavor is, coffee, and I say for crying out loud *why*, it's a flavor you can drink all day long, it's nothing *different*!"

She had really become rather violent. Cliff was grinning at me, and I began to laugh. Although he was my immediate boss, he didn't talk much shop here. It was usually these mock-grave discussions of subjects like food and murder mysteries. I said, "What used to be my favorite was hot butterscotch sundaes with maple walnut ice cream."

"Aha," he said. "Now that's something I haven't tried."

I said, "I worked in a dairy bar summers, when I was in high school. I tried everything, it was free."

"I was a milkman summers, but all I could try was milk."

"Chocolate milk?" Kaykay asked.

Out the window, the sky above the football field was deep October blue. An autumn day, the chilly mornings, the warm sunny afternoons. The weather had changed to autumn right after Labor Day, as if this year Labor Day signaled Nature, also, to get back to work.

And so must I, back to my classroom and pronouns and twenty-three general freshmen. Suddenly I was almost physically sick with yearning for my days at Thornhill, the hours at the typewriter, the shirts I ironed, the floors I mopped, the meals I planned and cooked. And yet. And yet my routine was nearly the routine of an animal, dark and unconscious and blind. At three thirty in the afternoons I would take a book and sit and wait for David to come home. Ann Turner, though no prettier than I and actually a year older and a guidance counselor, of all things, must have seemed, by contrast, alive.

I said, "Have you tried jogging?"

Valerie, the practice teacher, looked up from the papers she was correcting. "You go jogging?" she asked. "Where?"

"At the park in Hull."

Cliff said, "I read the book about it and that completely exhausted me," and took out his pack of Pall Malls. "Would you like one, Emily?"

"Thank you," I said. He lit it for me. I always hated to have my cigarettes lit, so David hadn't. I inhaled. "Wow," I said, instantly reeling. I picked up the *Saturday Review* he'd brought in. "May I?" I looked at the ads in the back.

He said, "Planning to leave us already?"

I laughed but didn't answer. TEACHING OPPORTUNITIES. AUSTRALIA WANTS YOU! JOBS! JOBS! HOUSEMOTHER FOR RESIDENTIAL SCHOOL. The ad I paused at said, "Manpower, Inc., needs experienced stenos, typists," and I thought again of what Warren had said about working in an office. If there was one thing I was, it was an experienced typist. But I had no shorthand or anything. Did you need shorthand nowadays, didn't they have machines?

And as I walked back to my classroom, along the pastel-painted cinderblock corridors teeming with hordes of pushing and yelling kids, I tried to picture myself living alone in Boston or New York, working in some office, and I couldn't.

"All right," I said to the class, "let's settle down." I opened the grammar book and waited, and while they settled I remembered being enclosed in the house we rented in Thornhill, snug, the snow above the windowsills, the furnace sighing warmth, the white winter sunlight in the kitchen.

I left school that afternoon more anxious than ever to get home and change and go to the park with Warren. In the rear-view mirror the school, long and flat and dreary, diminished. I drove past little houses, most of which had Virgin Mary statues on their lawns with sometimes in the fallen leaves a floodlight to show her off at night. Millbridge was very French Canadian, more so than Saundersborough, but Saundersborough was enough French Canadian to make me quite capable of pronouncing and spelling my students' names, because they were names of friends I had grown up with. Beauchesne. Duquette. Marcoux. Pelletier. Vachon. And, of course, my brother-in-law was John Ouellette.

Main Street was the most miserable one I'd ever seen, and although I hoped I might come to feel affection for its ugliness, as I was beginning to with Hull's, I hadn't yet and doubted if I would. The smell of the mills and the tannery. Drab stores along the polluted river. For some reason I glanced up, and in this Main Street the surprise was intensified, the surprise you get after seeing only, knowing only, the downstairs façades of stores as you walk or drive past and then one day you look up and see windows, curtains, a geranium, a face. A fat old woman sat in a window, watching the cars below.

There were more little houses on the way to Hull, and Millbridge became Hull where apartment buildings were being constructed in a field. Milkweed pods had blown white. There was a shopping plaza, and the Miracle Mile. It was rather like being always a commuter, I thought, this living in Hull and working in Millbridge and going to a class in Durham, or was it like being a displaced person? Displaced from David.

• • •

The running cleansed; it was impossible to think about anything else but the exertion. Beyond the park, cars sped along the turnpike. By the last lap I was gasping and my eyes and nose were streaming and I had to slow again to a walk.

"Come on!" Warren bellowed. He'd already finished, and, tall in sweatpants and sweatshirt, leaned against the bus. "Let's get it down to nine and a half minutes this time!"

Christ, I thought, and broke into a jog. I'll never make it, I'll never make it.

"Slave driver," I wheezed when I reached the bus. I took a Kleenex out of a pocket of my Levi's and blew my nose. "Well, did I do it?"

He was watching a green MG which drove slowly past the tennis court. "What? Oh, near enough, you'll do it tomorrow." He handed me the towel he wore around his neck and I wiped my face; I'd learned to take off my eye makeup when I changed after school because it smeared so with tears.

He said, "Want to go to Dot's?"

"Okay." I climbed up into the bus, and, still panting and sweating, put on my jacket and buckled my seat belt. To have a beer afterward seemed a cancellation of some of the benefits of the running, but it was Warren's habit and I usually went along.

"Beautiful downtown Hull," he said as we drove up Main Street. It was a very crazy main street, complicated by being two one-way streets, so when you went shopping you had to study your errands carefully and then plot a route to keep from going around and around. Perhaps it was the annoyance of this that made the citizens of Hull drive like maniacs. We charged up the one-way branch which curved between the old brick factories on the river, and we jounced to a stop at the red light. The shoe factory was letting out. Tired thin men, hard-looking women in slacks, heavy women in kerchiefs and long coats, and young girls, chattering and laughing, moved along the crosswalk.

Then we had to turn and drive down the major branch of Main Street. The stores had lit their neon signs, but despite the brave pinks and greens and golds the street was gray and bleak. We drove past Adele's Dress Shoppe, a Western Auto, Stan's Submarine Sandwiches, Cohen's Shoe Store, St. Pierre's

Bakery (TRY OUR CANADIAN PORK PIES!), a loan company, Bert's Supermarket, Claire's Card Shop and Light Lunches, Woolworth's, and turned again and drove down a little side street. Factory housing, old brick duplexes, gray paint flaking on the clapboards of apartment buildings.

The unlit sign over the door of a tall crooked brown house said THE HI HAT. It came on just before Warren opened the door, so we were greeted inside by the sight of Dot's broad bottom and sturdy legs as she climbed down from the booth seat she'd used to reach the switch. I was interested to see that she wore panty hose instead of a garter belt.

"Hi there, kiddies," she said, smoothing her flowered dress. "How many minutes today?"

"Almost nine and a half," I said. "I'll never ever make it in six minutes," which was what Warren ran it in, "and I'll never ever run it without stopping."

"Sure you will," Warren said.

The place wasn't too busy and noisy this time of afternoon; today there were just a couple of guys in a booth and three at the bar, UNH kids, all familiar faces by now. It was a cold room, the walls and battered wooden booths painted dark brown long ago, the ceiling brown from cigarette smoke, the dirty linoleum on the floor almost entirely worn through, but after a few visits it began to seem warm and homey. If, that is, you ignored the state of the bathrooms: I had been once to the ladies' room and ever since I had controlled the need until I got home, and Warren said the men's room (it had no running water, except the men) was the most unforgettable he'd ever known.

Dot said, "Well, I think you're nuts, I wouldn't let this idiot talk me into doing such a thing," and she beamed affectionately at Warren and, large and solid, she tramped into the kitchen for our beers. We climbed onto barstools. There was a Kold-Draft system behind the bar, but for years Dot had served only bottled beer and she'd never rearranged things, in case she changed her mind and started serving draft again, so she had to fetch every beer from the kitchen we could see through the serving window behind the bar. Since there was nobody to hand the beers to through the window, she had to tramp back out and around to the bar carrying them. She plunked our Buds down and automatically reached for the two Planters Dry Roasted Peanuts packets we always wanted, and picked up the dollar Warren had laid on the bar. She sold potato chips and pretzels, too, and sometimes she made a sandwich for a kid or offered a serving of her supper. This afternoon she was cooking something in the kitchen which smelled lovely, something with peppers.

"How is it out?" she asked, taking her own bottle of beer from under the bar.

I said, "I can never tell after running, I'm too hot."

"It's nice out," Warren said. "What you should do is you should get one of these bums here to mind the store and come run with us."

"Ha!" she shouted, and lit a Chesterfield. She was a friend of Warren's folks, had known him since he was born, took pride in telling me how she'd served him his very first beer here when he was at least five years underage, and it was through her and her talks with him that I'd begun to learn some of the things I couldn't bring myself to ask outright. He'd been in the army after high school. Then he got a part-time job at WHNH and went to the university for a year, decided he liked WHNH better than UNH and went to work full time. He had become the Morning Man three years ago.

She said, "You ought to've seen the way I was running around this place last night, my Christ, was it busy. No wonder I feel so shitty today."

"Tell you what," Warren said. "We'll get you a pedometer and see what you clock."

The burly kid at the end of the bar who was writing something on a paper towel glanced up. "Okay, Dot, I've got that down, chuck roast, onion soup, one small can of mushrooms. What comes next?"

"It's onion soup *mix*," she said. "One envelope Lipton's onion soup *mix*, the dry stuff."

"Oh," he said, and made a note. His hair was so long some of it had snagged under the neck of his tie-dyed T-shirt.

"Then you take a piece of aluminum foil," she said, "and put the roast on it and sprinkle the soup mix all over it, dry, remember, dry, and dump the mushrooms on top and wrap it all up good and tight. Got that?"

"Uh-huh," he said, scribbling. "Then what?"

Onion-soup pot roast, she was telling him how to make an onion-soup pot roast. David had loved onion-soup pot roast.

She said, "Then just stick it in the oven at say about three-seventy-five degrees and cook the hell out of it, an hour and a half, two hours. That's all there is to it."

I ate a peanut and looked up at the television on the shelf. It was a color set, but the program was *Candid Camera*, black and white. A car with a *Candid Camera* woman at the steering wheel was pushed into a gas station when the attendant wasn't looking, and then the woman told him her car wouldn't go and he opened the hood and there was no engine. The guys beside us began to laugh.

Dot said, "Isn't that the limit?" and belched comfortably.

The attendant said, "Lady—"

"But I have to get to work," the woman said, "can't you do *some*thing to make it go?"

"Now look, lady—"

We were distracted by the door's opening; almost everyone always turned to see who was coming in. This time it was Valerie, the practice teacher, whom I'd never noticed here before.

"Valerie!" Dot cried. "Where have you been keeping yourself, it's been—" and she stopped.

Valerie hoisted herself smoothly onto the stool beside me and draped back her heavy curtain of long dark hair which had swung forward. "Hello there, Miss Bean."

"Emily," I said, feeling a hundred.

She said, "I've been working, Dot. I'm practice-teaching over in Millbridge."

"That's right," Dot said from the kitchen, "it's math, isn't it?" She brought Valerie a beer.

On the television the car was being pushed surreptitiously into another gas station. I ate my last peanut and looked at the clutter on the counter behind the bar, the bottle of catsup, the jars of mayonnaise and mustard, the copy of the *Hull Courier*, Dot's knitting, a grandchild's toy panda. Dot was a widow; I wondered, as I wondered about my mother, if she were ever afraid to look in the mirror in the evenings. But of course she and my mother had their children, and my mother had her schoolchildren, and Dot had all the kids who drank here.

Warren said, "Want another?"

I glanced at him. It was rare that he suggested more than one. "What the hell," I said, "it's Wednesday, the week's half over. That's something to celebrate."

Dot said, "It sure is easy to see you love your work, Emily," and went to the kitchen for the beers.

I ate peanut crumbs. "Tonight I have to correct two sets of general freshmen quizzes on pronouns, is that something to love? Then I've got homework I should do for my class tomorrow night."

But Warren was having supper with me tonight, so first there'd be the lamb chops to cook and the salad and the coffee to make, and then after we washed the dishes we would sit, very domestic, in my little antimacassared living room and he would watch *The Glen Campbell Good-Time Hour* and *Room 222*, which was about a high school, while I partly watched them and partly did my homework, and then we'd go to bed. And I wouldn't be alone and nothing, I'd be semen-drenched and scotch-scented under my landlady's satiny turquoise bedspread.

Candid Camera was over now, and we drank our beers and watched some of an old *Perry Mason* show. A guy and girl came in and started playing the pinball machine. Dot, strangely silent, put on her glasses and picked up her knitting and sat down on the stool behind the bar.

I looked up at Warren's profile, and something about it made me realize he wasn't seeing Perry Mason and Della Street at all.

"Well," he said. He drained his bottle. "You about ready, Emily?"

"Okay," I said, and finished mine.

Dot said, "All set, kiddies? Take care," which she always said to everybody leaving. But as we went outdoors into the afternoon-changed-to-evening, into the smell of smog and autumn, it seemed to mean more. There was a green MG parked behind the bus. Was it Valerie's, did Warren know Valerie? Had she been the girl at the election-returns party? I felt blind panic.

• • •

Susan said, "But soy sauce doesn't go with turkey."

"I would like some, please, however," Pam said. She was five, and helping us set Susan's table for Thanksgiving dinner.

"Well," Susan said, taking the bottle out of the cupboard and giving it to her, "I suppose it'd be like chicken chow mein. Sort of." She opened the silverware drawer. "How many are we?" she asked herself absently, and then she seemed to remember that we were one less this year, for her roundish face flushed very pink as she counted out five forks. She wore her light-brown hair drawn back and fastened at the nape of her neck with a thong, and she looked like a Madonna.

It had been like this ever since I arrived, Susan too careful of what she said and too wary of what Pam might say. I knelt down and patted Bruce, the border collie, who was lying in the middle of the kitchen floor right in the line of our traffic. Then I noticed Pam. "My God, Susan, Pam's *drinking* it!"

And she was, head tilted back, swigging soy sauce.

"I know," Susan said, glad of the diversion. "She likes it. She also eats bouillon cubes."

I said, "At least it's not a sweet tooth."

"She's got that, too," Susan said. "Once she wanted ginger-bread and sardines for breakfast, didn't you, you foolish child."

We all three laughed. I got up and looked in the oven at the turkey whose golden-brown fragrance filled the entire house and even overpowered the smell of the plants—the hundreds of plants which made walking into Susan's house like walking into a greenhouse, humid and lush.

It was about an hour's drive from Hull to Cate. I had timo-rously driven up this morning, one of St. Pierre's Bakery mince pies on the seat beside me. The road was frightening because it was fairly straight, so Massachusetts drivers still turnpike-dazed drove it far too fast, racing north; no doubt it would get more and more fast and busy as the ski season progressed. I must, I decided, figure out a back-roads route.

Sandy soil and pine trees. Billboards advertising motels, ski areas, ski shops. Then Mount Chocorua above its little lake, very beautiful. I was in the White Mountains now, but on the wrong side of the state and the wrong side of the national for-est, not on the Connecticut River side which to me was the proper side because Saundersborough was there and, farther north, Thornhill. Yet the feeling of being up in the clouds was the same, the air was as clear, and I rolled down the car window and breathed it, icicle-sharp.

Everything was more barren over here, however. Cate was on a high plateau overlooked by mountain crests, not snug in the green river valley like Saundersborough and Thornhill. I came to the motels promised by the billboards; the roadside grew crowded with gift shops, restaurants, art galleries, antique shops, which Saundersborough and Thornhill had escaped until now because they weren't quite close enough to the ski areas. Now new ski areas and A-frame developments were being built there.

Then I came to the main street of expensive clothing shops and coy country stores and real-estate offices with colonial façades. I drove past the brick high school where John, Susan's husband, had taught math until this year, when he had become the assistant principal. I drove over a carefully preserved covered bridge, and down a long farm road. On the land between the rambling old white farmhouses many cheap little houses had been built, and some trailers had moved in, and, most recently, weekend skiers had put up A-frames and chalets. Susan and John's rented house was one of the cheap little houses, a yellow one, looking as temporary as the trailer next door on the flat pastureland.

Postwar plywood, David used to call it. But rents were high in Cate, and the rent for this house was comparatively inexpensive, so Susan and John had found themselves staying on and on; this was their fifth year in it.

Now Pam said, "I do believe it must be time to eat, Susan."

"Not yet," Susan said, and Bruce barked and jumped up.

John called from the living room, where he was sharpening the carving knife out of the way of Pam and Bruce, "Your mother's here."

I looked through the plants in the window and saw Lucy's pale-blue Volkswagen parked behind my car in the driveway. Lucy got out, and, laden with paper bags and a pie basket, came up the walk. We hurried outdoors, Bruce barking and jumping and wagging.

Lucy said, kissing Pam, "Good heavens, sweetheart, you smell like soy sauce."

We unpacked things in the kitchen, and John, who was short and tough and startlingly good-looking, with tight curly black hair and long curly eyelashes, began making martinis out of the gin and vermouth one of the paper bags had contained. And there was a bowl of Lucy's homemade cranberry sauce (David was free of that now, too, and probably having the canned jelly kind which he preferred; were he and Ann spending Thanksgiving with his folks or Ann's folks right now? Where did Ann's folks live?), and there was a homemade pumpkin pie, a bottle of olives, and some canned goods obviously grabbed from Lucy's pantry—beef stew, deviled ham, ravioli. Lucy was so used to her daughters and sons-in-law being poverty-stricken on teachers' pay that she continued to bring provisions with her when she visited and to slip us a ten-dollar bill when she left; it was a practice she'd begun when her own teacher's pay hardly permitted it, and now, although teachers' pay was beginning to be nearly like other people's, it was a habit. We accepted it, because money was no longer a worry to her since her parents died.

We sat in the living room peering at each other around large plants and sipped our martinis while Pam lay on the floor with her crayons and paper, drawing weird pictures and swigging soy sauce.

"You've moved the sofa," Lucy said. "I think it was better where it was."

Ever since Pam was born we had had Thanksgivings and Christmases in Cate. This was rather a relief to Lucy, who liked cooking special goodies but hated cooking entire meals. While we were still in elementary school, Susan and I were getting the breakfasts and suppers and packing our lunch boxes. Lucy, when inspiration struck, made things like cream puffs or apple chutney.

She was sixty-two, and no doubt would go on teaching until she was seventy; she loved it, and she loved little kids. She had taught six years before she met and married Ned, our father. Ned was still at Dartmouth then, and Lucy had moved to Saundersborough and taught there, living with my grandmother, Ned's mother, in the white house on the tree-shaded street, and after Ned graduated and managed to find a Depression job in a sawmill, they all lived in the house. My grandmother died. There was no money, only the house, the beautiful house slowly declining, and they stayed, and I was born, Susan was born, the war was on, and Ned worked in a factory converted to defense. The war was over and Ned had a good job at a ski factory and I was eight and Susan was six, when the lumber on a flatcar he was having unloaded shifted and crushed him and two of his men to death.

Susan said, "I had to move the sofa. I had to change this room *some*how after five years of its hideousness."

"How about painting it?" Lucy said.

"It'd still be wallboard."

Lucy said, "You haven't found a house yet?"

"You know how it is around here, the prices are fantastic for anything we'd want."

Lucy said, "It's getting that way everywhere," and crossed her nyloned legs. She always dressed very formally. Today she wore a suit of a color that was probably called toast, with a blue blouse the color of her eyes, always oddly innocent behind her glasses. Susan and I, in slacks and sweaters, felt, as usual, dowdy beside her, fashionably bell-bottomed though we were. Not only did Lucy wear this sort of clothes to school, but she also kept them on at home, girdle and all. I had seen her in full regalia, dress, earrings, brooch, heels higher than any I could bear, bustling around the kitchen, making dandelion wine.

John said, "But still we like this neck of the woods and I like my job, so there's no point in moving, is there?"

"No," Susan said, smiling her deceptively serene smile, "no. I'd better go check the kitchen."

"May I help?" Lucy and I said together.

"Thanks, but I think everything's under control."

Lucy said to John, "If you find the house you want, the down payment, as I've told you—"

"Yes," John said, "and we thank you."

On the desk in the corner, over which a heavy pot of begonias hung from the ceiling rather unnervingly, I could see piles of books about plants, and stacks of magazines and newspaper clippings. Some would be about Susan's dream: a greenhouse and a shop.

"Well, Emily," John said, "how do you like teaching?"

I hesitated, and then realized I didn't have to worry about hurting his and Lucy's feelings. "I don't like it," I said. "I don't like kids, and it all seems one hell of a waste of time."

"How's the school?" John asked.

"Oh, it's the way most schools are, I suppose, there's not enough money, and the administration sort of gropes along, and everyone's gone mad from the dullness, so there are ferocious battles in teachers' meetings about the dress code or gum chewing or the number of sick days."

John laughed. Lucy said, "You're still writing, aren't you, Emily?"

"No," I said. I looked again at Susan's desk and dream. In Thornhill my dream had been fame and fortune and posterity. It had also been a farmhouse on a back road, which someday, when David's pay went up a bit more, we could buy somewhere in Thornhill.

"Darling," Lucy said, "you know you can always come home and spend all your time writing, you know that."

"Yes, thank you," I said, although of course I wouldn't and she knew it. Two things I'd been certain of: I wouldn't take alimony from David, and I wouldn't live off Lucy any longer than I had to while I hunted for a job. Even those months had been too long for me, back once more in my girlhood bedroom where I had begun. The small white bed, the dressing table with the pink-and-blue chintz skirt made by Lucy's mother, the desk where I had written my first stories, done my homework, written letters and letters and letters to David.

Susan came in, and Pam presented each of us with a drawing. "Why, thank you," we said. Mine seemed to be of Bruce, interpreted in purple.

John said, "You wrote that you go jogging with a Morning Man?"

During the time of the divorce, it was John who was the easiest of the family to be with, maybe because he wasn't family or maybe because he was John, matter-of-fact, sure of himself and of things. So was Lucy, but she was my mother.

"Yes," I said, "he's a nice guy. I bought a radio; it's kind of eerie, you know how you listen to announcers and without realizing it you begin to picture what they look like from their voices, or at least I do, and then when you once in a while see a photograph of them in the newspaper or somewhere, you're all wrong. With him, it's backwards, his voice is wrong, it doesn't sound the way he does in person."

There had been no more encounters with Valerie at Dot's, and everything was just the same, the running and the evenings together; I was sheltered. But, I told myself, for God's sake stop talking about him.

Susan and Lucy seemed rather embarrassed, wondering what to say next. John said, "How about another round?"

With the second martinis, work in the kitchen became hectic, mashing turnips, mashing potatoes, making gravy, buttering boiled onions, pouring wine. We all grew irritable, as usual, including Bruce whose tail got stepped on. And at the last minute, as usual, John wanted pickles and relishes like his mother used to serve at her Thanksgivings and which Susan always forgot; Susan told him to get them himself, and, very silent, he opened the refrigerator and took out jars and spooned their contents into little dishes. He remembered to use the good china.

Then we were sitting, and there was calm. John began to carve the turkey. We admired the kitchen table transformed by one of Lucy's mother's damask tablecloths and her white-and-gold Limoges plates. The food smelled frantically delicious. I tried to think of something I'd give thanks for if there were someone to thank. Oh, you selfish bitch, think of the kids starving in Biafra, belly buttons popping out of distended stomachs. It's the food you give thanks for, and that today you can forget calories.

Lucy said, unfolding her napkin, "This reminds me, Susan, are you through with Ma's diary so Emily can read it?"

"Diary?" I said. Ma was Lucy's mother; unable to pronounce Grandma and Grandpa when I was little, I had called her folks Ma and Pop. Ma's real name was Emily. She had died two years ago, and Pop had died a year before her.

"Yes," Susan said, and then jumped up. "I forgot the celery!"

Lucy said, "You know how it is, there was so much stuff from Ma and Pop's house I still haven't gone through all the cartons. But when I was sorting out one, I found a five-year diary Ma kept, it's quite fascinating, nineteen-o-five, six, seven, eight, nineteen-o-nine. When Susan and John came visiting last time I gave it to her to read and she'll pass it along to you."

John raised his glass of wine. "Here's to us."

Pam spilled her milk.

●　●　●

The howl of an ambulance woke me up late on a Saturday night, and as I lay there trying to sort it out of a dream about some long senseless search, I realized it had stopped on this street and I got out of bed. The linoleum was sleekly cold under bare feet.

My bedroom window overlooked only the dark yard between this house and the next. Without turning on lights, I walked through the kitchen into the living room and peered out the window.

The streetlights made everything silvery pale. The ambulance was parked behind my car, and men were loading a stretcher into it. Then the howl began again, and they were gone.

I turned on the kitchen light and poured myself a scotch, and went back to the living room and stood, trying to hear what voices were saying what downstairs. After a while, Mrs. Dupuis's old Chevrolet drove out of the garage. The house seemed suddenly very quiet.

Warren hadn't come over tonight. He hadn't phoned.

I turned on the television and watched a Barbara Stanwyck movie which I was sure I had seen when I was a little girl munching popcorn at a Saturday matinee in the smelly Saundersborough movie theater. I had another stronger drink.

So I was slightly headachy the next morning, and I decided I would be brave and drive to the ocean for fresh air. And on my way downstairs I was brave enough to stop at the second landing. Behind the Dupuises' door, they were speaking rapid French. I knocked. Mrs. Dupuis, short and plump and wearing a flowered smock which made her look even rounder, opened the door.

I said, "I'm sorry to bother you, but I heard the ambulance last night—"

"It was Mr. Crabtree," she said, switching smoothly into English but retaining her accent, "he had a heart attack. I went to the hospital to be with Mrs. Crabtree, none of their children live around here, you know."

"Is he—"

"He passed away."

"Oh, no, how awful."

"She's sleeping now, they gave her something. I got hold of the oldest son, down in Massachusetts, and he'll contact the others and they should get here sometime today. Except for the daughter in California, of course."

"I'm so sorry. Tell her I'm so sorry."

"I certainly will, Emily. Everything all right up in your apartment?"

"Oh, yes, it's fine," I said, wondering how much she'd noticed Warren's visits.

Outdoors, the fat old beagle wheezed as he waddled painfully across the faded lawn.

I drove along the turnpike until I came to the Portsmouth exit, and then the route signs led me through town. We hadn't yet got much snow in Hull, and most of it had melted; here at the seacoast there was hardly any at all. Would the entire winter be like this, not like the thick heavy white winters in Saundersborough and Thornhill?

The marsh grass was vivid orange. Ice had shrunk the pond in front of our honeymoon cabin colony, and the free water was crowded with ducks and geese and swans. The empty beach looked so cold I couldn't believe I had ever sunbathed on it. Six miles out on the horizon the Isles of Shoals were sharp and clear. The Seaside Restaurant, I saw as I drove past, was still open.

And, thinking of Mr. Crabtree, of whether he had died while I was watching that old movie or later while I slept, I drove too far and suddenly realized I was nearing Ma and Pop's camp. But something was wrong; the road was wrong. Had I gone crazy? Then I saw a sign that said OLD OCEAN ROAD. So this was a bypass across the salt marsh behind the camps, and I had a choice, I didn't have to see it after all.

I heard my directionals begin to click. I turned and drove down the Old Ocean Road which had been simply the Ocean Road when we stayed here. There it was, a shabby gray cottage above black rocks.

I parked the car on the little gravel driveway and got out. But the salt air didn't blow my headache away; it seemed to increase it. The gray ocean became white spume as it dashed itself against the rocks.

I was here, yet Ma wasn't here to open the door and greet me.

Ma and Pop didn't own the camp. It belonged to friends, and Ma and Pop rented it for a month each summer and drove up to it from Lexington, Massachusetts, and Lucy drove down from Saundersborough with Susan and me. We stayed the entire month then, but while Ned was alive we stayed only the two weeks of his vacation from the factory.

No matter how hard I tried, I couldn't remember much about being here with Ned. I wanted to remember everything. I could remember his helping Susan and me in our solemn searches for shells and starfish and sand dollars and white pebbles. I remembered our helping him dig clams. And I remembered how he would build a fire on the rocks and how Susan and I would stand avidly by to watch him put the lobsters into the boiling kettle; fascinated, we watched the lid scuttle about after they were dropped in. And I could remember one time when Susan and I were playing in the waves at the beach and we were suddenly caught in an undertow. We went churning around, choking up the ocean, terrified, and then there was Ned, hauling us out.

He was very handsome and young-looking, even to us. He looked so much younger than Lucy that once one of the kids on the beach thought he was our brother, Lucy's son. Susan and I found this uproariously funny; Lucy hadn't.

In the summer the stone wall in front of the cottage was pink with roses.

I tried to see myself, years ago, sitting on that black rock there, longing to be grown up and do splendid things.

I got into the car and drove back to the bypass. When I was fourteen, the trips to the camp became too much for Ma and Pop; they stopped renting it and stayed home summers, and grew older.

In Ma's diary now they were engaged, both of them working at stockbrokers' offices in Boston. Ma lived in Concord with her father; her mother had died when she was a child. Pop lived in Lexington with his folks.

• • •

Tues., January 3, 1905. Rain and then blizzard. Worked until five thirty train. Bought Chester (who was Pop) a watercolor for his birthday. Chester and I printed pictures and played cribbage in eve.

Mon., January 16, 1905. My sweetheart's twenty-fifth birthday. May he be as well and happy when he is seventy-five.

Tues., January 31, 1905. In eve all of us girls went to Mrs. Stewart's and had a linen shower for Betty. Had lovely time.

Thurs., February 9, 1905. Concord Dramatic Club gave *Saffron Trunk*. Very good. Lost my glasses on way down in the snow.

Sun., February 12, 1905. Sewed on red waist in A.M. Chester came up in P.M. and bro't me dish and half dozen plates for a valentine. Began to snow hard in P.M.

Mon., February 13, 1905. Chester had a holiday, so he went to Old Howard in P.M.

Thurs., May 18, 1905. Chester came up in eve and cut out medallions for me and I sewed on white dress.

Sat., May 27, 1905. Went to Chester's to spend Sun. He and I played three sets of tennis in P.M. Went to dance at Old Belfrey Club in eve. Jessie, Malcolm, Chester, and I went down to hot dog cart and filled up.

Sun., May 28, 1905. Went picking Solomon's-seal in P.M.

Wed., June 14, 1905. Walked to lawn party with Chester. Gorgeous moon.

Thurs., August 17, 1905. Chester came up in eve. Bro't me some sweet peas. They are my favorite flowers.

Wed., August 23, 1905. Busy stock market today on account of rumors of peace between Japan and Russia. Poor Chester over in the exchange alone.

Sun., August 27, 1905. Made sponge cake, salad dressing, and applesauce in A.M. Chester came to dinner as his folks are in Methuen. He drew me some designs for pin cushions, and I sewed braid on checked skirt.

Thurs., August 31, 1905. Chester's folks offered him their house for twenty-five dollars a month rent, they paying us seventy-five dollars board, netting us fifty dollars on which to run the house and fifty dollars, his salary, to live on. The house can't be fixed over this or next year, and I don't want to be married until I can have a bathroom. It is too embarrassing.

Wed., September 6, 1905. Mr. Atkinson offered Chester position in their Butte, Montana, office. Urged him to go. Must decide at once. Hard for us both to do. He came up in eve and we talked it over and decided it best for him to go if his mother is willing, which I doubt.

Thurs., September 7, 1905. Chester's mother thinks he ought to go to Butte, so he will go. We all feel terrible that he must go but it seems the only thing to do. He can come back in three or six months if he doesn't like Butte.

Fri., September 8, 1905. Chester settled with Mr. Atkinson. Goes to Butte next Wed. Mr. A. said he could come home and get married when he got ready. It breaks my heart to have him go. It's the hardest thing I ever did. If I could only go too! Butte has thirty-five thousand people. George Fisher was awfully discouraging about it. Other people not so bad.

Sun., September 10, 1905. Went to church, then to see Aunt Sally. In P.M. called on Jim Moody. Saw man who has been in Montana. Very encouraging. Richard Palmer to supper. Down to Isabel and Sam's in eve. Also Malcolm, Jessie, Florence, Will, Ellen, Henry. Conversation vile.

Mon., September 11, 1905. Went to work. Went to call on Coles and Morrisons, then down to Jessie's. Chester went to Lawrence to spend day with his relatives there.

Tues., September 12, 1905. Chester went to Boston, got his ticket & two hundred dollars. He was awfully blue. I came home in eve and he came up. He seemed better and I felt better too. I must brace up thro' tomorrow. Mr. Atkinson told Chester he would at least double his pay. He was very nice to him.

Wed., September 13, 1905. Chester left at three thirty for Butte. His folks, Mrs. Morrison, Mrs. Perkins, Richard Palmer, Will, and I went down to train. He was in much better spirits than he has been. Do hope he will like it. Came home at four o'clock. Went down to Mabel's in eve and sewed while the rest played bridge.

Mon., September 18, 1905. Had *seven* communications from Chester—two letters from Chicago, one on train, two postals, private wire of his arrival in Butte, box of Allegretti's chocolates from Chicago. Do wish I knew how he is tonight.

Fri., September 22, 1905. Letter from Chester from Butte. Very favorable and quite enthusiastic. Do hope it will all continue. Ellen and Jane came up in eve and played cribbage with Priscilla and me.

Mon., October 2, 1905. Cloudy. Three letters from Chester and two papers. Sewed in eve. Went to bed at nine o'clock.

Mr. Atkinson decided to give Chester one hundred dollars per month to begin on.

Tues., November 21, 1905. Went to Betty's. Fifteen there. Wrote letters to Chester, wrote poems, guessed baby pictures, etc.

Tues., November 28, 1905. In P.M. had telegram from Chester. "Good news. Atkinson says spring OK. Cheer up." Oh, I'm so glad. I wonder what month it will be.

Tues., December 5, 1905. Worked till five forty-seven train. Sewed in eve. Went to bed early. So tired. Got Chester's letter yesterday enclosing Mr. Atkinson's and saying he would come when I told him to. I said last of April.

Wed., December 6, 1905. Took my sewing up to Mary's in eve. They were playing bridge with Aunt Sally and Uncle Gordon. I told them I was going to be married in the spring.

Sat., December 9, 1905. Lend-a-Hand Fair in P.M. Bot lots of things for my house. Sewed with Mary in eve. *First* snow of the year.

Sun., December 17, 1905. Sewed at Kitty's all day and at Priscilla's in eve on centrepiece for Aunt Sally. Don't know whether I can get it done or not, and I'm so tired I'd like to throw it in the fire.

Mon., December 25, 1905. Pa gave me ten teaspoons and two serving spoons that were my mother's wedding presents.

Sat., January 6, 1906. Went up to Miss Hubert's in P.M. and arranged about her making my muslins. Snow squall.

Thurs., January 11, 1906. Worked until five forty-seven train. Sewed in eve. All my table linen and sheets came. Sent Chester ten dollars in gold for his birthday.

Thurs., January 18, 1906. Miss Hubert sewing for me on three muslin dresses. Church supper in eve. Chester wrote that he wanted to be married earlier than May 1.

Sun., January 21, 1906. Almost 70° out and just like spring. In P.M. walked on Robinson's Hill with Henry, Nell, and Philip. Henry stayed to tea. I worked on my wedding list. Six hundred names already, counting Mr. & Mrs. as one.

Tues., January 23, 1906. Temp. 65. Got telegram from Chester saying he preferred to be married April first, so I've set the day as the third. Ten weeks from tonight.

Wed., January 24, 1906. Finished wedding list in eve. Decided to have seven or eight hundred wedding bids and three hundred and fifty reception cards. Cold—25° at nine thirty P.M.

Mon., January 29, 1906. Went up to Aunt Sally's in eve and hashed over reception list. Cut it down to two hundred and ninety.

Sat., February 10, 1906. Went to oculist in P.M. Got to have stronger glasses. Telegram from Chester saying Mr. Atkinson says April 3 OK.

Tues., February 13, 1906. Rained hard. Sick. First time on date exactly for years. Wonder if I'll squeeze thro' April 3. Seven weeks from tonight.

Wed., February 21, 1906. Went to club to hear Griggs lecture on Tolstoy. Small crowd as it poured hard all eve. Lecture good—sat with Isabel and Sam. Quit work forever, I hope.

Sat., February 24, 1906. Fine warm day. Sewed all day with Jane and came back to Lexington in eve. Chester's father home from Europe. Brought me drawers, chemise, stockings, gloves, and picture.

(Lucy now had the diary Pop's father had kept during the trip. Once at Ma and Pop's house I had curled up on the old sofa and read it.)

Thurs., March 15, 1906. Priscilla had euchre party in P.M. for me. Thirty-six there. Fine time. Snowed hard all day. Regular blizzard. Went to bed at eight thirty.

Tues., March 20, 1906. Chester came on three o'clock train. I went down to his house to supper. He seems just the same. Oh, I'm so glad he's come.

Thurs., March 22, 1906. Aunt Sally had ten girls to lunch for me—Jessie, Betty, Priscilla, Ellen, Jane, Isabel, Babs, Kitty, Nell

& Florence. All went to tea at four at Mrs. Stewart's to meet Miss Townsend. Chester up in eve.

Tues., March 27, 1906. Chester and I went to Boston and bot our rings at Stowell's.

Wed., March 28, 1906. Luncheon and cards at Mrs. Bates'. Took first prize at euchre. Euchre party for me at Jessie's in eve. Twenty-eight there.

Thurs., March 29, 1906. Tried on wedding gown in A.M. All finished. Concord in P.M. with Chester. Party for us at Staffords' in eve. Played hearts.

Mon., April 2, 1906. Packed. In P.M. went down to Priscilla's to supper. Jessie and Florence there. We four went to ride around State Road by moonlight. Then rehearsal at church. Perfect evening. I do hope tomorrow will be like it.

Tues., April 3, 1906. My wedding day! Elegant day, warm & clear. Married in Lexington Unitarian Church by Mr. Reed at eight P.M. Went to Boston to Lenox Hotel and spent night.

• • •

I stopped the car beside the pond and looked at the ducks and swans. David and I had got married in April, too, during the April vacation of our sophomore year at Brompton. We were married at home in Saundersborough, in the living room, by a lawyer who was a justice of the peace and who was also a friend of Lucy's. Lucy was there, and Susan, and David's folks, and Ma and Pop had come up on a bus because they didn't like to drive anymore.

After the quick ceremony, after the drinks and canapés and kisses, David and I had left and driven to the ocean to spend three nights, which was all we could afford without dipping too deeply into wedding-present money that must be saved for tuition and the mysterious expenses being married would bring, like electricity and fuel. This cabin colony was new then. Which cabin had it been? There was a small living-room-and-kitchen, with a window overlooking rocks and sea, and at the general store down the road we'd bought supplies, bacon and eggs and hamburg and beer, officially a married couple at last, going shopping, and I cooked our first meal in our own place in that kitchen. When we weren't in bed we walked along the rocks or went for drives, and we visited the cottage, closed for the winter.

Then the last afternoon I did a wash and hung it out on the little clothesline. David's honeymoon-new white wool socks weren't dry by evening, so I laid them across the grating of the gas floor furnace, and we went to bed.

We woke together. He said, "There's something wrong," and the blackness was choked thick with gray, but I was sleepy and slow, I didn't understand, and then he said, "Jesus H. Christ, the place is on fire," and he dived across me, yanked me out of bed, threw my bathrobe at me, and pulled on his pants.

In the living room we found it was just smoke, the cabin filled with smoke from the charred black socks on the register.

David managed to pry them off while I opened windows, and we began to laugh. Yet later, with the years, the memory became much more frightening than the moment had been. We could have suffocated. It could have ended then, if we hadn't awakened in time.

• • •

The night before the night before Christmas, and here I was at Dot's, drinking beer and smoking one of her cigarettes. Although the track at the park was covered with snow now and Warren and I no longer went running (he did stationary running in his apartment, but I couldn't in mine without annoying the Dupuises beneath me), I still came here often after school for there was never any awkwardness about being alone and female; sometimes when I was here with Warren he was the only male in the place, sitting with me at the bar lined with UNH girls. I could quite clearly imagine, if there were boys and they caused any trouble, Dot's charging out of the kitchen brandishing a bung starter.

She sat on her stool behind the bar, wearing a muumuu, cardigan, and slippers, putting pre-tied ribbons on Christmas presents and scribbling names on Christmas tags. "Going home for Christmas?" she asked.

The place was nearly empty. Most of the kids had already gone home. I was the only one at the bar. "No," I said, "to my sister's up in Cate. She has the holidays there since my niece was born, it makes things easier. I wish Christmas didn't come so soon after Thanksgiving, it's too exhausting to see family again so soon."

But what would I do if I didn't go there? Just what I'd been doing so far this vacation, working on my project for my Improvement of Reading course I'd chosen, mistakenly thinking it'd help me help my students, and correcting papers, and waiting for Warren to phone, which he hadn't. It was to escape this that I'd come here tonight.

We'd had supper Friday night at the Pizza Hut and then had gone to his apartment. I hadn't heard from him since. Today was Tuesday. It seemed much longer.

I said, "At least Susan doesn't have turkey again. We never had turkey on Christmas even when we were kids." (David's mother always cooked a turkey on each occasion.) I picked at the damp label on my beer bottle. "My grandparents would come up to our house for Thanksgiving, but on Christmas we'd go down to their house and we'd have steak. Eggnog was the big thing, though, we'd open the presents and then my grandfather would make eggnog. My sister and I had to have plain eggnog until we were sixteen; it was quite an occasion the first Christmas we could have a cup of grown-up eggnog."

I was asking Dot how she celebrated, did the children and grandchildren gather in the never-seen living room somewhere in this tall brown house and when did they open presents and what did they eat, but she slapped another ribbon onto another package and just said, "Jesus, do I hate doing this, I'll never get them done, I feel so shitty," and took a swig from her beer bottle.

When Pam was born, holidays were so much an ordeal for Ma and Pop that Lucy and David and I had the Christmas tree at Susan and John's and then we all drove down to Lexington to visit briefly. There was no eggnog, no tree, and instead of beribboned presents there were checks written by Pop in a trembly hand. There were illnesses, too, and a sense of mourning; it was all over but for shadows. Then, after Pop died, during the last Christmas visit a stranger was in the house, a Mrs. Wright, a "companion," who cooed at Pam and Ma equally. Lucy wept, and once more tried to convince Ma to come to live in Saundersborough, and Ma momentarily became Ma again, saying firmly she would die in this house. And she had.

Dot said, "I like Bing Crosby, do you like Bing Crosby?"

"Yes," I said.

On the television was the annual rerun of *White Christmas*, with Bing Crosby and Rosemary Clooney, appallingly awful but pleasantly nostalgic, for I could remember seeing it in that smelly theater when I was fifteen. And it was very pretty, red and white and green.

I was fifteen when David and I started dating.

"Oh, God," Dot said, "I can't remember who this one's for." She held up the holly-figured package. "I wrapped the damn things this morning, but then I started making Christmas cookies and I didn't have time to put on the bows and tags. I can't even remember what it is, what the hell do I do?"

"Open it?" I suggested.

"*Think*, Dorothy," she told herself, and lit a cigarette and glared at the package, while Rosemary Clooney and Vera-Ellen sang "Sisters" on the television.

A year ago tomorrow night David and I had been at Susan and John's, and David and John were drinking beer while Lucy and I helped Susan dig out Pam's presents from hiding places and arrange the packages under the tree. I was, for a change, feeling safe; this familiar ritual soothed the worry of what was the matter these past months with David. As usual, David and John bitched the familiar bitches about school, and as usual David ate the grubby peanut butter sandwich Pam had ceremoniously made for Santa Claus, and when David and I went to bed we slept on the cheap fold-down sofa which was so narrow that we had to cuddle close instead of lying apart tense and silent as we had been doing at home.

"Damn it all," Dot said, and ripped off the wrapping paper and opened the white box. "Oh. Of course. It's for my daughter-in-law." She unfolded a pink nightgown. "Do you like it?"

"Yes, it's beautiful," I said, although it wasn't.

She contemplated it through cigarette smoke. "I think it is, I think she'll like it. I'd like one myself."

I wondered for whom she'd like to wear it, and the door opened and we turned to see who'd come in.

"I'll be damned," I said to Kaykay Harrison and Grace Fifield.

"Exactly," Kaykay said, climbing up on a stool and arranging her armload of store-wrapped presents on the bar. "We were just talking about you, we were just going to phone you. Two Buds, please, Dot."

Grace said, "And a bag of those pretzels."

Kaykay said, "Why don't you have some potato chips, too, while you're at it?"

Grace made sure Dot was in the kitchen and whispered, "She doesn't have any Wise potato chips, they're the only kind I like."

"Go ahead," Kaykay said, "rub it in."

Grace was indeed thin; her straight legs below her green Loden coat reminded me of Raggedy Ann's. Her brown hair was set in a dull medium-length hairdo, and the frames of her glasses were pale brown, not assertive horn-rims or even silly round gold-rims. She was one of those girls you knew in high school, and you never expected them to get married and were always surprised when later you learned they had, usually to someone as plain as they. Grace, who was about thirty-three, had not got married.

Dot came out with the beers, her slippers shuffling, and said, "Where's Bob tonight, Kaykay?"

"I made him stay home so I could buy him his Christmas present. He borrowed a tuba from the school during vacation, and he's practicing. I'll bet the people upstairs over his apartment just love it." Bob taught music at Hull High School, and I'd gathered that when he and Kaykay weren't arguing about the merits of coffee ice cream they were arguing over which school had the honor of being worse, Millbridge or Hull.

"What'd you get?" Dot asked, always interested in purchases. I'd had to open bags and display a new dress, new shoes, a scarf, and underpants, on various occasions.

"I got him a Waterpik, you know those things you spray in your mouth," Kaykay said. "He has trouble with his gums and the dentist said he ought to get one but of course he never bothered. And it's something we can both use when we're married."

On trips to Saundersborough and Lexington, I packed one toothbrush, and David and I both used it.

"Then some stuff for my folks," Kaykay said. "I'm going home tomorrow."

Dot said, "Where is it you're from?"

"Brompton," Kaykay said, "God help me."

I said, "I went to school there."

"I went here," she said, "probably because I was born there. Look how long Rosemary Clooney's skirt is. Do you think we're really going to have to wear them that long again?"

"I'll refuse to," I said. "I'll start wearing pantsuits to school instead, and get fired. You were going to phone me?"

Kaykay said yes and lit a Salem. "The thing is, we're fed up with our apartment, and Grace got looking around for someplace else to move into when I leave this summer, and she found one she liked so much she had me look at it and I practically started packing that night. I'd rather spend the rest of the year there than in our hellhole. But the rent's pretty high, a hundred and eighty a month—"

"Jesus Christ," Dot said, slapping on another ribbon.

"That's what all these new apartments are asking, or more. Anyway, we figured if we split it three ways it'd only be sixty bucks each, and heavens, right now we're forking out fifty-five each, so it wouldn't be much of a jump for us, and for you, Emily, it'd be a saving, wouldn't it?"

Dazed, I said, "I'm paying eighty."

"See what I mean?" Kaykay said.

Grace said, her voice calm after Kaykay's, "It's that group of new apartment buildings on the way from Hull to Millbridge. They've finished this one and just started renting."

"Where the milkweed was?" I said, and the door opened, we turned, and Warren and Valerie came in.

O tidings of comfort and joy.

"Well, kiddies," Dot said. They sat down in a booth, and she went into the kitchen for their beers.

Grace said, "Would either of you like a pretzel?"

"Thank you," I said, taking one. He must have seen my car parked outside; this then was a declaration. I hoped the blood flooding into my face didn't make it so red as it felt. You are not going to throw up, I told myself, and you are not going to leave. I unclenched my jaws enough to eat the pretzel, swallowing carefully to keep from choking.

In the taut silence, "Goodness," Kaykay said to Dot, who was behind the bar again, "look at all those Christmas cards."

We looked; Santa Clauses and angels looked back at us out of the cards standing on the Kold-Draft. There was a big stack of envelopes on the ancient cash register which sat atop a pile of empty beer cartons.

"From all over," Dot said. "You know, the kids who've graduated and gone away. There's so many I haven't even gotten around to opening half the damn things." She glanced at me and went into the kitchen.

Kaykay said, "It has wall-to-wall carpeting. Gold. And all the kitchen stuff, the refrigerator and stove, they're avocado."

"On the house," Dot said, plunking down a beer for me and a pile of Christmas cookies in a paper napkin. "Fresh made today, help yourselves."

There were bells and stars and wreaths dusted with red and green sugar.

"Dot," I said.

"That's all right, you'll be all right."

I said, "You know what I bought my niece for Christmas? A couple of turtles. I bought them too early, though, a week ago, I knew I should've waited, I've got *attached* to them. I've even given them names, Aggy for the aggressive one and Timmy for the timid one." I bit into a green star. "Hey, delicious, Dot. Well, what's just occurred to me is how the hell do I get them to Cate?"

Dot and Grace and Kaykay all jumped on the conversation offering. "Are they in a tank?" "A bowl?" "Put it in a box on the car floor." "Won't they get cold and freeze?" "Put it near the heater." "Put it over the tailpipe"—from Dot. "Where's the tailpipe?"—from me. Kaykay said, "I wonder if you should take the water out, they might get seasick."

Then Grace said, "Do you have a lease on your apartment?"

"No."

"Neither do we," Kaykay said, "so I guess we're all set. Aren't we?"

I was trying to think of it and not of Warren sitting over there, tall, his smooth dark hair and silky sideburns. Christ, I thought, it'd be like being in school again, with roommates, or would it be a Hull attempt at the life shown in slick movies about girls living in New York, nylons drying in the bathroom, the telephone constantly ringing, and cocktail parties? Then I thought of going home now and climbing the stairs through the supper smells from Mrs. Crabtree's and the Dupuises' apartments, to my dark apartment and my homework and the turtles. What was the point of it, what was I doing here? And no Warren anymore. Alone. I thought of the mirror.

Kaykay said, "Aren't we?"

"Give her time," Grace said. "There's the moving to consider, all the packing and everything."

I said, "I haven't got much to pack," and ate a red bell. "All right," I said.

THE ROOMMATES

"IF WE had a bottle of champagne," Kaykay said while around us people jabbered hoarse through cigarette smoke, "we ought to break it across a corner of the building."

We had a great many things on the coffee table, on the end tables, on the kitchen counter, but we didn't have any champagne. We had scotch and bourbon and gin and beer, however, and all the goodies Kaykay and Grace and I had shopped for in the morning and spent the afternoon preparing, the sort of goodies I used to look at pictures of in magazines and clip out recipes of and save for the parties David and I never could afford to give.

Dips and spreads, potato chips, corn chips, cheeses and crackers, shrimps, cocktail sauce. The preparations had been frivolous and fun, arranging cherry tomatoes and mushrooms and cucumber slices around a bowl of sour cream, making a pretty pattern, ignoring the knowledge that the pattern would be ruined the moment someone took a piece; it had been like playing house.

And this was a housewarming party, or rather, as Kaykay pointed out, a building launching. Ours, a downstairs apartment, was the first apartment to be rented. And so far the party was quite a success, with teachers and their wives or husbands getting cheerfully drunk, and Bob, Kaykay's fiancé, playing his guitar.

"When I consider," Cliff Parker, the head of the English Department, was saying to the French teacher, "when I consider the phases of my life, I find that they are marked by the automobiles I've owned. My résumé is a junkyard."

"It takes a worried man," Bob sang very loudly, "to sing a worried song." But he didn't appear at all worried. He was overweight and jolly, and now, because of the heat of the room and his exertions and the drinks, his face had a glazed baked look, like a round pink plate.

A science teacher said, "Did you hear the one about the woman who'd been married three times and was still a virgin?"

"How could she still be a virgin?" someone asked dutifully.

"I'm worried now," Bob sang, "but I won't be worried long."

"Well, her first husband was a psychiatrist, and he just talked about it, and her second husband was a gynecologist and he just looked at it, and her third husband was a gourmet."

Somebody's cigarette scorched my arm. I turned and saw Cliff Parker.

I said, "Speaking of gourmets, I had the weirdest dream the other night about the Galloping Gourmet french-frying yards of toilet paper for a women's liberation group to throw at some personage in protest."

"It'd be a disconcerting attack, wouldn't it?" he said. "How do you like this place?"

"Well," I said, and looked around. The little kitchen was separated from the living room by a Formica counter for which we'd bought barstools whose plastic-cushioned tops unfortunately made embarrassing noises when you sat down on them. There was the avocado-green refrigerator and stove Kaykay had promised. And in the living room was the gold wall-to-wall carpet. The walls themselves were white. "Well," I said again.

Most of the furniture was Grace's. It was traditional, and the sofa and chairs all had skirts, even the ottoman had a skirt, and everything matched, a print of blue and cream. I'd been bored by it the minute I saw it, and now it was simply objects to sit on.

But Grace's choosing this style was somehow pathetically poignant, especially her bringing it to this bleak new brick-faced building surrounded by cement mixers and piles of girders and the beginnings of other identical buildings rising from the snow-crusted ravaged earth. She wanted tradition; she was not camping out, as Kaykay and I were; she was making a home.

"Well," I said once more. "At least we don't have to sweat yet about the noise annoying anybody upstairs."

Bob sang, "Twenty-nine links of chain around my leg."

I said, "Sing the verse about the little bitty hand waving after me, that's Pete Seeger's favorite verse, I heard him say so on TV."

"You watch his show?" Bob asked, pausing to take a swallow from his highball glass.

"Of course I did, while it was still on, and when it went off I nearly wrote the station a vicious letter, but I never seem to get around to writing any of the vicious letters I want to. Pete Seeger's my hero," I added, and then realized what I'd let myself in for. Chatty Emily after too many drinks.

"Hey," he said, "that's right, Kaykay told me, where's that banjo of yours?"

Cliff said, "You play a banjo?"

Drunk enough not to be coy, I headed for the bedroom, ducking lifted elbows, dodging cigarettes. Grace was picking an olive pit out of her philodendron.

Kaykay and I shared the larger bedroom; Grace had the smaller all to herself. Their old curtains didn't fit these windows, so it'd been necessary to go shopping for some; Kaykay and I chose yellow and purple flowers to compete with the white walls, and Grace chose rose organdy. It'd also been necessary for me to buy a bed, the first single bed I'd slept in, except when I was staying with Lucy during the divorce, since I got married. I had bought a second-hand bureau, too, and a cheap yellow bedspread like Kaykay's. Grace had an antique-white Heirloom bedspread.

I took the banjo out of its case and went back to the living room and snaked the ottoman away from a math teacher who'd left it unguarded to get some bleu cheese dip.

"I'll play 'Cripple Creek,'" I announced, and sat down and did so. The sharp crackle of noise momentarily deafened everyone into silence, and I grinned at them, not in the least flustered by having an audience, although I hadn't played at a party since Brompton. And although I hadn't played much at all lately, only a couple of times for Warren and once for Grace and Kaykay and a few times for myself when the excitement of the songs could make me forget singing them with David, my fingers remembered and it went fast and crisp. "Now," I said, "let's do 'Worried Man' again," and Bob and I sang, "I looked down that track just as far as I could see, little bitty hand was waving after me," and I wondered if I'd begun to regress or what, first the make-believe of the party preparations, and now this, which was like being back in high school, or at Brompton before we got married, being once again Emily Bean who played a banjo.

"Whew," I said, "would you like to play it?" and handed it to Bob. "I've got to get a drink."

In the kitchen, people on their hands and knees were patting at the floor.

Joanne Webster, the art teacher, said, "Have you seen a contact lens anyplace, Emily? I lost a contact," and Kaykay, crawling across the floor, looked up and said, "Are you sure you didn't swallow it? I knew somebody once, it fell out in their drink and they swallowed it."

Joanne said, "No, I didn't swallow it, I'd know it if I swallowed it."

Grace said, "You're sure you lost it here, not in the living room?"

"I burned one once," Joanne said. "I took them out to go to bed and one stuck to my finger and when I put out my cigarette it fell in the ashtray and I put the cigarette out on it, but I never swallowed one."

An English teacher said, "If it's in the living room, it's a goner."

"Here's a smoked oyster," someone called from behind the wastebasket.

"Maybe it *was* the living room," Joanne said, and in the living room Bob sang, "I know a girl in Boston, Mass., she has freckles on her ass."

"Oh, God," Kaykay said, "he's gotten to the dirty-songs stage." She scrambled to her feet and seized a tray off the counter and swayed slightly. She apparently had also reached a stage. The tray tilted; a sardine flopped off a cracker. "Sardine, anyone? Bob," she called, working her way through the people toward him, "Bob, wouldn't you like a nice sardine?"

He was playing his guitar again, and the banjo was lying on the floor by his chair, so I rescued it from the danger of feet and carried it into the bedroom.

After I'd put the banjo back in the case, I took Ma's diary out of my top bureau drawer and opened it to my bookmark. I shoved aside the coats piled on my bed and sat down, and, by the dim light of the tiny hallway, I read: "Sun., May 13, 1906. Our first dinner party! Mr. and Mrs. Spencer the guests. I cooked everything & it was fine—chicken soup, lamb (roast), gravy, scalloped potatoes, asparagus on toast, fruit meringue, coffee."

Down the hall the toilet flushed. I heard footsteps and someone humming a TV commercial, and when I looked up I saw that Cliff had stopped by the open door. "Double-good Doublemint Gum," he hummed, and focused his blue eyes on me. "Emily. Are you all right, is anything wrong?"

"No, no, just having a little quiet."

"Would you like a drink?"

"Got one, thanks," I said, holding up my glass. But the thought of a cigarette occurred to me, and it seemed a very pleasant thought. "Could I perhaps bum a Pall Mall?"

He came in and gave me one and lit it for me. Then he pushed aside more coats and sat down. "That looks like rather an old diary."

"It's my grandmother's." And because he was boozed-up and informal, not in a suit but in a turtleneck and plaid bell-bottoms, just as I was, and with his brown-and-gray hair and beard all curly and tousled, I forgot he was my boss long enough to risk being foolish and confide, "She's been married about a month and a half and she's giving her first dinner party," and I read him what she'd cooked.

For a little time we smoked in silence.

Then he said, "Not exactly clam dip, is it?"

"No," I said, and stood up and got an ashtray off Kaykay's bedside table and sat back down and flicked off a curve of ash. I'd suddenly wanted to touch his beard. I'd never touched a beard before, and I'd suddenly wondered if it were like pubic hair. Shock at myself became amusement; I laughed and said, "They're out in Butte, Montana, and it's nineteen-o-six. They went out there right after they got married, and they stayed four years, and when they came back home to Lexington they lived the rest of their lives in the house that had been my great-grandparents'."

Kaykay went past the door, on her way to the bathroom, and saw us and waved. In the living room Bob was singing, "It's me, it's me, I'm home from the sea, said Barnacle Bill the sailor."

Cliff leaned back against coats. "My grandparents never made it as far as Montana. They lived all their lives in the same place, and so have my parents, just about. North Riverton."

Which was near Thornhill. I said, "I'll be damned, I lived in Thornhill eight years. Small state, isn't it?"

"You did, did you like it?"

"Oh, yes, well, I—"

We both stubbed out our cigarettes and took a drink.

He said, "What I want most is to go back and teach there."

"It's not a particularly whoopee neck of the woods for a bachelor."

"Oh, I could have an occasional fling at the Riverton Inn if it hasn't collapsed from dry rot by now."

"The Riverton Inn," I said, "for heaven's sake, we once stopped there for a beer. We. That is—" If I was beginning to be able to mention him as a figure in my life, what could I call him? Ex-husband? Good God. "The guy I used to be married to," I said at last, and thought that David was not simply a figure in my life but the main part of it, the main part of all my memories, all my history.

Cliff glanced at me as if he wanted to ask something, but apparently he too shied away from direct questions, for he said instead, "I'd like to get back up there and enjoy it during the time we've got left before the entire state becomes one great big playground full of Massachusetts tourists."

Kaykay went past again, returning from the bathroom, and waved again.

I said, "The reason I'm down here is to pick up some credits at UNH." I was asking him why he was here.

He said, "What a fate," and offered me another cigarette. "I went to school here and stayed on and got my master's, to get everything over with all at once." While he reflectively tapped his cigarette before putting it in his mouth (might his beard or mustache catch on fire if he smoked it too short?), I swiped his matches and lit my cigarette. He said, "I'm here because I was offered head of the department and I was too greedy to resist. It at least got me back to New Hampshire; I'd been teaching in Massachusetts for years."

"Oh," I said.

"Pepsi's got a lot to give," he hummed. Then he reached over and rumpled my hair. "Hey, I thought so, it's shorter than mine."

I touched his beard. It felt as tough and wiry as a Brillo pad. Then he kissed me, and we were lying among the coats. The booze said yes, but I said no.

"Our cigarettes," I said, struggling to sit up, "we'll burn everyone's coats and get sued."

He laughed, and we sat up and I flicked ashes at the ashtray while he put out his cigarette. Fleetingly I wondered where he lived, if we could go there, and then I remembered he was my boss and this was impossible. I wasn't brave enough to sit at department meetings and discuss gerunds and *Julius Caesar* with him while everyone guessed we were sleeping together.

"And anyway," I said, not realizing I was saying it aloud, "I'm never getting involved with a man ever again," and I finished my drink and stubbed out my cigarette.

"What, never?" Cliff said.

The Gilbert and Sullivan response came automatically. "Well, hardly ever," I said, and he kissed me and his hand was warm on my breast.

Luckily at that moment I heard Bob. "Roll me ooover," he bellowed, "in the cloover."

"Oh, Jesus," I said, starting to laugh, and I jumped up and opened the banjo case and said, "I'm going to drown him out. Any requests?"

"How about 'It's Hard, Ain't It Hard'?" he suggested as he lit a new cigarette.

"Sorry about that," I said, laughing, "I'm sorry."

I ran into the living room and sat down on the floor and began to play.

• • •

Grace and I usually spent Friday night alone watching television, while Kaykay cooked supper for Bob at his apartment and then stayed overnight with him. Kaykay and Bob were already very organized about their sex life, something, I realized, David and I had never been, especially after my change from diaphragm to Pill. We had been exuberantly spontaneous, sometimes embarrassingly so, like the time at Brompton the bed broke one sunny afternoon when wives and children from the other apartments were sitting and playing in the front yard right outside our open bedroom window.

This Friday night in February, Grace and I were watching *The Name of the Game* as usual, and then she suddenly put down her dish of strawberry ice cream and said, "I ought to go see my sister, I haven't seen her since we moved here and of course she can't get out much because of the kids."

I said, "I didn't know you had a sister." I only knew she had parents she ate dinner with every Sunday.

"Oh, heavens, I've got two sisters. The one I was thinking of is Wendy, she's the youngest, she's twenty-one. Sort of a mistake, I guess. All Mom's friends were pretty horrified when they found out Mom was pregnant at thirty-four." She smiled at me, but we were both thinking that here we were, thirty and thirty-three, not even having begun on children and unlikely to.

I offered, "My mother didn't get around to having me, her first kid, until she was thirty-two. She had my sister when she was thirty-four."

Grace went into the kitchen and rinsed her dish. "My other sister, Norma, is a couple of years older than me. Her husband is a salesman at Glidden Ford, that's where I bought my car. They've got a nice house in that development on the Hull Point Road. And they have a daughter who's a sophomore and a son in junior high. Bob knows the kids." She dried her hands on a dish towel. "All in all, I have five nephews and nieces."

"Wow," I said.

She said, "I met Norma in the dry cleaner's last week and she told me she's started going to a ceramics class Thursday nights."

I watched her push back her cuticles with the towel and then squirt hand cream out of the dispenser bottle on the sink counter into her palm.

I said, "I suppose ceramics might be fun. More fun than Analysis of Teaching," which was the course I was grimly taking this semester.

"Well, she says it gets her out of the house."

But Grace wanted desperately to be in a house.

Rubbing her hands, she laughed and said, "For a while, whenever I saw Norma all she did was ask me if I had a boyfriend and if I was getting married, and she used to get so mad at me for being bridesmaids and maids of honor in other people's weddings, she used to say, 'You're not going to be in another wedding!' She really believed always-a-bridesmaid-never-a-bride, can you imagine? Nowadays when I see her she tells me how lucky I am to be out in the world doing things on my own. Out in the world! Millbridge High School!" and she laughed again.

During these past couple of months I had begun to sense the great hurt in Grace, far greater than her composed appearance and neat habits suggested. Despite her furniture, Grace was not resigned to her life and never had been.

She said, "I did get some lovely dresses out of all those weddings, and I've even worn a few of them again, for chaperoning and banquets and things. Were you ever a bridesmaid?"

"No," I said. "I was away at Brompton when my high school friends started getting married, and none of my Brompton friends had a real wedding. Are weddings a good time?"

"Some of them, and they're always so pretty. The dresses—would you like to see the dresses?"

We went into her rose-and-white bedroom. She opened her closet, pushed aside school clothes, and brought out garment bags.

"This one was a winter wedding," she said, spreading a green velvet gown on the bed, "and this was Norma's wedding, and this was a friend's in high school, and this was my roommate's at Plymouth, and this was Wendy's, and here's the latest, when I was maid of honor for the girl I roomed with before Kaykay."

And there they were, the green velvet, the chiffons and satins and silks, yellow and pink and lavender, all flowing across her single bed.

"I shortened the one from Wendy's wedding and wore it to the senior dance last year with the fellow I was going with then."

Kaykay had told me that he was a social studies teacher who had moved on to Rhode Island. His replacement was married, so there was no replacement for him in Grace's life this year.

Grace slowly began to hang the gowns back in the bags. "Isn't it awful?" she said. "Forty or fifty dollars for each one, and only a few of them I've ever worn again, such an awful waste," but her hand stroked chiffon and silk.

She said, "Would you like to come along? To Wendy's?"

I thought of the rest of the evening alone with the television. "Why, yes, that'd be nice."

We put on our coats and got our pocketbooks and went out to her car. It was a dark-red Mustang which she took to an automatic car wash every Sunday morning. It gleamed in the night. I hadn't yet found the courage to try to drive through a car wash or even to go to a do-it-yourself one, so the battle David had fought to keep the salt on the roads in winter from rusting out the Falcon was beginning to be lost.

Grace drove very calmly and competently. Kaykay drove her Volkswagen too fast and impatiently. And I myself still drove in a constant state of terror, seeing myself smashed dead by every oncoming car.

The rains this week had washed most of the snow away, and the days had seemed almost springtime, with the earthy smell of spring, and the grass yellow-green. Now the night was a false spring night, moist and foggy.

I said, "Up in Thornhill, we'd still be trying to shovel ourselves out."

We turned at a dairy bar closed for the winter and drove along a sad road of ramshackle little houses selling snowmobiles or second-hand furniture or home-baked bread. In used-car lots, bright plastic streamers hung lank and wet beneath floodlights. The drive-in theater's marquee told us, CLOSED FOR SEASON, COLD'S THE REASON.

Grace said, as if continuing a conversation of explanation in her head, "You'll wonder, she's so young and three kids, but she had to get married when she was sixteen."

"Oh," I said. I wanted to ask whether or not her trousseau had been maternity clothes.

"My folks, it just about killed them, they kept trying to find excuses for it, but really they blamed themselves. They shouldn't have, it's one of those things that happen."

"I'm sorry."

"But they're fine now, and they dote on the babies, and they helped Wendy and Arthur with the down payment on the trailer. Arthur's a nice boy, Arthur Thibodeau, and he works at the Hull Textile Mill. They manage somehow, even though he doesn't make much money, and the trailer's lovely, I was astonished at how big trailers are. Wendy keeps it spick-and-span, despite the kids. Here we are."

The sign said WHISPERING PINES MOBILE HOME PARK. I couldn't see any pines, whispering or silent; I could see just rows and rows of trailers, windows glowing behind curtains. A strange world.

And I couldn't imagine how Grace identified the trailer we stopped at, except by the old Chevrolet parked beside it. The trailer seemed to be aqua, but so were many others. Grace went up the steps and knocked on the storm door, which had aluminum curlicues on its glass window.

"Grace! Come in, come in!"

It was impossible that Wendy was Grace's sister. She was fat. And her fatness wasn't only the broadening of hips caused by childbirth; it was also teenage plumpness solidified into married stoutness. But above the distorted body in bulging slacks and straining blouse, Wendy's face was smooth and young and pretty, her long dark hair carefully brushed.

"Well, hello there, Grace," Arthur said, getting up from the sofa where he was lying watching the end of *The Name of the Game.* "Where've you been keeping yourself?" Taller than Wendy, he looked slight beside her, except for the beginnings of a paunch.

"You know how it is," Grace said, "I've been meaning to come over. This is Emily Bean, she's rooming with Kaykay and me at the new apartment."

"How do you do," I said, glancing around the living room. I had never been in a trailer before. Although it certainly was bigger than I'd expected, I felt distrustful of its size, suspecting things hidden away inside other things; the place made me nervous.

Wendy's style was also traditional, a sofa and two matching chairs in brown-and-orange tweed. Was this trailer-traditional?

"I know," Wendy said, taking our coats, "and I've been meaning to phone you some afternoon. Want to see the kids?"

I didn't, because I never knew what to say to or about kids, but I followed her and Grace past the room divider of brass poles on which philodendrons (slips from Grace's?) climbed, into the kitchen where the refrigerator and stove were avocado like ours and everything shone. Wendy hung our coats over the back of a vinyl-cushioned dinette chair and we went on down a hall. I was beginning to feel slightly claustrophobic.

Wendy opened a door, and we peeked in at a couple of little boys asleep in little beds. "Tommy is four," she told me, "and Toby is two."

"Aren't they cunning," I said inadequately.

"I want to get them some new bedspreads," she said. "I thought maybe a plaid, or maybe sailboats on them or something. I've been looking at the Giant Store."

She turned to a partly open door, and we went into a tiny bedroom. A baby slept in a crib. My usual dilemma: Was it a boy or a girl?

"A girl at last," Wendy said, solving the problem. "Theresa. She's four months."

"Isn't she cute," I said. "And all their names start with *T*."

Grace didn't say anything. She leaned over the crib. The mobile of plastic birds swayed gently.

I didn't want a baby, I'd never wanted one, there had simply been once in a while a certain curiosity to see what David and I would look like mixed up together. But Grace, I realized, wanted a baby.

On our way back to the kitchen, I looked through an open doorway into the big bedroom that evidently was Wendy and Arthur's. Above the bed hung a haloed picture of Christ. But Grace wasn't Catholic; Wendy must have converted. There had been no such situation when Susan and John got married, for

John hadn't gone to church since his altar boy days, and Susan, like me, had never gone to church at all. Their wedding had been the same as ours, the lawyer and the living room, canapés and drinks.

In the kitchen Wendy said, "Should I make some coffee? Or how about some tonic? There's Coke and some diet stuff."

What I longed for was something alcoholic.

From the living room Arthur called, "How about a beer, Wendy?"

So Grace and Arthur and I had beers, and Wendy had a bottle of Diet Pink Grapefruit. "I'm always trying to lose," she said, as Grace and I sat down in the tweed chairs and she sat down beside Arthur on the tweed sofa, "but I never can. Arthur likes his potatoes, and I'm just miserable if I'm sitting there without one watching him eat his."

I said, "Kaykay and I have to watch Grace. It's agony."

"That's Grace," she said, dismissing the phenomenon of Grace's metabolism. Then she lit a Winston and said, "When you see Mom and Dad next time, Grace, could you kind of hint that what I want for my birthday is one of those electric cooker-fryer things? I've been wanting one for ages but I just can't afford it. You can do lots besides frying in them, you can cook spaghetti sauce and heaven knows what. Norma has one. Of course, I need new towels, too, that's the trouble with getting all your sheets and towels all at once at your shower, they all wear out together. I'd like some sheets, too. Permanent press. They've got them at the Giant Store and the Mammoth Mart." This, I gathered, was a hint for Grace.

On the coffee table stood their wedding photograph in a silver frame. Wendy wore a long white gown. Her pregnancy didn't show; she looked plump and pretty. Arthur looked sheepish. Beside the photograph were two champagne goblets, gleamingly polished, but the white satin ribbons had yellowed.

I felt suddenly trapped, as if now that I was in the trailer I couldn't get out.

I said, "Could I bum a cigarette?"

"Sure, go right ahead," Wendy said, and continued, her voice sliding voluptuously on, "Next payday I'm going to buy a new dress for Theresa, I know it's silly, I've got all the clothes that Tommy and Toby wore, but they're boys' clothes and I'm just so sick of them and seeing Theresa dressed up like a boy. What I'm going to buy is a pink dress, with lace trim. Hey, I almost forgot!" she said. "We took some more pictures, get Grace the album, Arthur."

She pronounced "pictures" as "pitchers," and when I had to check myself from correcting her I was nonplussed by my English-teacher reaction. Good God, was I actually becoming one?

Arthur fetched the photograph album from the shelf of the brass-plated television stand. On the television screen, in *Bracken's World*, a Hollywood world, starlets quarreled.

Grace looked at the pictures thoroughly, slowly turning the pages, and Wendy came over to comment on them. "We've cut Tommy's hair since then…those are the snowsuits Mom and Dad gave them for Christmas, remember?…I don't like that one of Theresa, I almost threw it away but Arthur likes it…aren't they cute, helping me give her a bath?"

Grace handed me the album, and I looked at round little boys crammed into matching snowsuits standing in the snow outside the trailer. After admiring the new pictures, I went back to the beginning and looked at pictures of the wedding reception, Wendy and Arthur cutting a tiered white cake, Wendy and Arthur feeding each other cake. Then there was Wendy in a maternity dress, then Wendy holding a baby in a christening gown, then baby pictures, then Wendy holding another baby who wore the same christening gown, and then there were pictures of babies and sand pails at the beach, of babies and toys under Christmas trees, of cakes with one or two or three or four candles, of Theresa in that christening gown.

I glanced up at Wendy. She seemed so happy. Could she really not want anything more than the wants she'd talked about? Could this really be enough? What would it be like?

"Well," Grace said, "it's getting late, we'd better head home. You come on over and see our place sometime."

We drove back toward what was left of the evening: I would have two or three drinks, watch television, in my bed I no doubt would masturbate, I might drunkenly cry.

I said, "She's happy, isn't she?"

"Oh, yes," Grace said, and didn't say anything more until we'd driven through our rubble of new buildings and parked behind our apartment. "It worked out very well," she said.

Indoors, I immediately got us each a scotch, and Grace made herself, perhaps for comfort, her favorite sandwich, canned sliced beets with mayonnaise. She turned on the television and we watched the eleven o'clock news, but I only saw it, I didn't hear it, because I was wondering what it was I wanted nowadays. I hadn't even tried to write; there was nothing but marking time.

I got up and went into my bedroom and took Ma's diary out of the bureau. In the living room again, I sat down and read, as the Johnny Carson show began, about her pregnancy with Lucy. Lucy had been born in Butte, three days before Ma and Pop's first anniversary.

• • •

Fri., March 29, 1907. Irene and her baby spent afternoon with me. Chester and I went for a short walk after supper. I felt fine. Went to bed at ten. Awoke at eleven and found the water in me had broken.

Sat., March 30, 1907. Lucy Martha born at eight A.M. I was sick nine hours. She weighed six lbs. Dr. and nurse say she looks like Chester but her coloring will be fair like mine. Everyone delighted.

• • •

I, sixty-three years later, went into the kitchen and made another drink.

• • •

"Come on," Kaykay said, sitting at the counter. She ripped an application form out of her typewriter. "I can't do another one, let's get out of here. 'Please state your philosophy of education.' What a batch of bullshit."

I looked up from my notebook. "I remember what floored me most was 'List any physical defects.' I wanted to put 'no head.'" The defect was of course a bigger amputation. No David.

It was a Sunday afternoon in March. Kaykay and Bob were already job hunting for next September, and I supposed I ought to be doing the same, but I couldn't bring myself to face what I'd faced this autumn alone, new town, new school, new apartment. Would I end up thirty years from now still teaching at Millbridge, one of those peculiar old-lady teachers living with another old-lady teacher? Lucy's example was no help, because she had us kids and the house and Ned's hometown.

Kaykay licked an envelope and said, "No head is perfectly right, sitting around reading your own diaries, you should be ashamed of yourself."

"I am, but it's become an addiction."

"Have a cigarette instead." She tossed me her pack.

"Thank you," I said, yet although I lit a Salem, I continued reading. The addiction had started one evening when, reading Ma's diary, I was reminded of the only diaries I'd ever kept, during a couple of years of high school, and I suddenly wanted to read them to go back to when I was clean and new. I found them, two notebooks, in the odds-and-ends drawer of my bureau, under the piles of manuscripts I ignored, under gloves and scarves and handkerchiefs and the beaded purse which once was Ma's.

And there, in the diaries, was David, the beginning of David.

• • •

Sat., February 19, 1955. Carol and I went down to the Girl Scout food sale to work from nine to one. Carol brought the sugar cookies her mother had made and I brought the banana bread I made last night. The sale was held in Bea's Alteration Shop—complete with no heat. One of the windows was broken, to top things off. So we almost froze. We took a break at about eleven thirty and went to Woolworth's. I had coffee and Carol had a Coke. Then back to the sale. Fred arrived at about one for Carol, and they gave me a ride home. The phone was ringing when I got indoors, and I didn't even take off my boots and jacket before I answered it. It was David Lewis! Would I like to go out with him tonight—plus Smitty and Mary Frances? WOULD I??? I was in bliss all afternoon as I lay on my bed reading *Four Years in Paradise*, by Osa Johnson. Susan and I made chipped beef for supper.

David and Smitty picked me up about seven thirty. Then we collected Mary Frances. And then we went to the movies. *Africa Adventure* was playing, and it was darn good, a film shot in Africa, but it was kind of embarrassing because the women in it didn't wear any tops. Next came the funniest movie I've seen in years. It was a horribly dramatic little number starring Joan Crawford, and funny! I nearly died. David didn't help matters any by making cracks at the most dramatic points. Smitty and Mary Frances were spellbound, and Mary Frances was even crying at the end, while David and I were practically rolling in the aisle. After, still snickering, we went to Nelson's Dairy Bar, and David and I had chocolate frappes. Then we went parking, in the parking lot of the Outing Club slope yet. David was really passionate—and he's so nice. Oh, I hope, I just hope—!! I got home at about ten of one.

• • •

Then all the many dates which followed, all the kissing and getting fresh, and all the words he said in parked cars, over the phone, and, after he'd graduated from high school and gone into the army, the words he wrote me in his letters. I had started to read the diaries casually, to see what I'd been like then, and I was concussed by the explosion of his words.

"I love you, I love you so…You're starting to drive me crazy…I'd love to marry you…I think you're the nicest thing there ever was…I'll always love you, always, no matter what happens…Dear Emily, I'm sorry that I didn't write you last night, but I missed you so much that I just couldn't think about you out loud."

Kaykay pounded stamps on envelopes and said, "You'll get yourself in a state, and I refuse to make you any martinis." Once when she'd found me crying in the bedroom she had fed me three martinis until I'd gone to sleep. She apparently preferred, as I did, booze to the sleeping pills Grace took.

I turned a page. From the vantage point of years, I was discovering the growth of David as well as the growth of our love, and trying to discover what had gone so wrong. Had he, instead of thriving on the love as I had, at last smothered?

"There," Kaykay said, giving a final pound. "Let's go do something."

Grace was away at her rituals of car wash and then dinner with her folks. Bob wasn't around, either; he was practicing his tuba at school.

"Do what?" I said. "What's there to do on a Sunday afternoon in Hull, New Hampshire?"

"Buy something," she said.

"Nothing's open."

"You idiot, all the discount department stores are open, one to seven. Haven't you ever noticed?"

"What's to buy? I don't need anything."

"Well, I do," she said, and got up and went into the bedroom and came back with a list. She had many lists of things needed before she and Bob could set up housekeeping, everything from double bed and mattress to eggbeater (Teflon). Gradually through the winter more and more items were being checked off as their embodiments were purchased and placed in the attic of the house where Bob had his apartment. It was somehow eerie; they were buying what David and I had bought and accumulated, the things which now were sold or distributed between the families.

Ma's diary said, after weeks of house hunting while living in a Butte hotel:

• • •

Wed., May 2, 1906. We looked at and rented cottage. Decided to move in Mon. Rent thirty-two dollars, including water rate.

Thurs., May 3, 1906. Mrs. Foley and I went to Mont. Hdwe. Store & bot stove, refrigerator, and other things and to Lander Ftre. Co. & got bed. In eve Chester and I went to Mont. Music Co. Got a Hallet and Davis upright piano for three hundred dollars.

Fri., May 4, 1906. Went to Hennessy's and bot dining set, etc.

Sat., May 5, 1906. Chester painted bedroom floor of our new house and we built our first fire.

Sun., May 6, 1906. Chester painted more and I scrubbed and we worked down to house all day. Went out to dinner.

Mon., May 7, 1906. Moved into our new house. Have to live in a mess till the floors get dry. Chester painted sitting-room floor. Slept in our own bed first time & got our first dinner.

Tues., May 8, 1906. Have to get up at six fifteen A.M. now. Chester gets up at six and fixes fire. I made white-flour muffins and they were good.

And on a memoranda sheet at the back of the diary was Ma's list:

May 3, 1906. Furnishings for House.

Range	$42.00
Refrigerator	12.00
Washbowl & pitcher	.75
Hammer	.50
Screwdriver	.35
Coal hod	.50
Shovel	.25
Teakettle	1.00
Broom	.50
Basin	.25
Dishpan	.25
Dustpan	.25
Bed	7.50
Springs	5.50
Mattress	15.00
Couch	3.75
Couch cover	1.75
Chiffonier	11.50
Mahogany table	12.50
One chair	4.00
One chair	11.50
Piano	300.00

• • •

"Come on," Kaykay said. "If I hang around here any longer I'm going to go berserk and eat Grace's steak, not to mention all her frozen chicken pies and her liverwurst."

My stomach growled. Kaykay and I were trying the "Inches-Off Diet," which meant no protein. I said, "I wonder what Grace is having for dinner at her folks'."

"Probably a ton of roast beef," she said, and threw my coat to me. "Come on."

Such a windy March, wild and high. There'd been a snowstorm last week, bad enough to have the school close early, but by now the snow was melted again, and the mounds of gravel and piles of bricks that had been white hulks were visible once more.

"Wow, this wind," Kaykay said as we leaned into it, walking around the building. There were a number of cars parked here; most of the apartments had been rented. She said, "Let's take my car, I'm a nervous wreck when you drive."

"So am I," I said.

We had to fight to get the car doors open against the wind. Kaykay's Volkswagen was a convertible, yellow with a black top, like a bumblebee.

I buckled my seat belt; Kaykay and Grace never used theirs. We jounced along the rutted sand, past cement mixers and stationary trucks, and we looked at the new buildings, judging, as we always did, how the work was progressing.

"Where to?" Kaykay said. "Let's try Hubbard's, I haven't been there for ages."

"Is that where I got my bedspread?"

"No, that was the Giant Store. Hubbard's is an awful place, but you can get a better deal on some things there."

It was on the other side of town, and the parking lot was crowded with cars. The turnpike screamed by overhead. The enormous dingy mill was old and weathered, and beside it flowed a brown river.

I said, "Hey, it's a real mill."

"It used to be, I don't even know what they made. I guess they turned it into a store years ago." We got out of the car. She said, "It always seems like every weirdo from miles around is here, and every female with her hair in rollers."

Many people were hurrying into the mill, and many people were coming out carrying bulky paper bags and howling babies. There were the women and girls with rollers either displayed quite naked or insufficiently covered with scarves or puffy pastel bonnets, there were mumbling old men, there were parents shooing along popcorn-eating children, there were lumpy old couples. Is this what people did nowadays on Sunday afternoons?

"Sure you don't need anything?" Kaykay asked as we walked along.

"I don't think so," I said. Then, "Well, razor blades."

"We can get them on the way out. Anything else? I wouldn't recommend their clothes, I never dare buy clothes in any of these discount stores. Do you? They're always made in Taiwan or God knows where."

"You're the social studies teacher," I said.

She hauled open the finger-smudged glass door, and we went up old wooden stairs worn shallow by how many years of workers and shoppers. Candy bar wrappers littered the corners, spittle speckled the steps.

Then Kaykay opened the inside door, and although the place was not one vast brilliant arena, like the shining new discount department stores, and although I had automatically steeled myself, I was assaulted here as there with such a kaleidoscopic abundance of goods that I felt my blinking rate slow down, and, dazzled, hypnotized, I followed her along the aisles of plenty, suddenly wanting to buy everything.

"Housewares," Kaykay said, walking briskly. Her gaze had hardened; she was bargain hunting.

There were big dark rooms here, a labyrinth of rooms over-flowing bath powders and men's shirts and children's paja-mas and ladies' print dresses. Gradually everything I wanted to buy began to seem tawdry, and my senses began to return. The rooms smelled of people and popcorn and of something else. Was it the sweat the workers had sweated here long ago, as the shoppers sweated now? The wooden floors were worn and crooked.

"This is it," Kaykay said, and we turned past racks of blouses and miniskirts (NEW SPRING COLORS!) into the glitter of aluminum. Kaykay marched on past pots and pans and halted at appliances, and there were Warren and Valerie, studying an electric toaster-broiler.

"Shit," Kaykay said. "I'm sorry."

"It's all right," I said, and, astonishingly, it was. I even was amused that they were looking at toasters; did this mean they were married, or getting married, or shacking up together? "Hi," I said.

"Hello, Miss Bean," Valerie said, pushing back her sweep of hair with her left hand, to show a small diamond engagement ring. "How's everything at Millbridge this semester?"

"As ghastly as ever," I said cheerfully.

Warren was the one who seemed disconcerted. He fiddled with the coiled cord of the toaster. "How's the jogging?" he asked in his in-person voice, not the radio voice we didn't listen to mornings, except when there was a snowstorm.

"I'm just dieting nowadays," I said. "We're on that no-protein diet."

Kaykay said, "It can't be very healthy, we'll probably die of something awful."

I said, "At least we won't die of scurvy."

"Waffle irons," she said, "that's what I'm after. There they are."

And we walked on, the display shelves offering us electric coffee urns, electric carving knives, electric frying pans, electric can openers, and, at last, waffle irons.

Kaykay said, "Her ring's got a nice setting, but I like mine better," and glanced complacently at her ring. "Now, the real stores are selling waffle irons for twenty-nine ninety-five. What are these? Twenty-two ninety-five, but, my God, I never heard of the brand names. Just what I feared."

"Does Bob like waffles?" I asked. David had loved them, and when we got married he had dug his mother's old waffle iron with the frayed cord out of the attic, and for years on Sunday mornings we had waffles.

"Oh, yes, and you can do all sorts of things besides on these new ones—pancakes and sandwiches and bacon and things. And they're Teflon."

I remembered Grace's sister Wendy. "Are you going to get one of those electric cooker-fryers? You can do other things in them too, or so I heard."

"Good Lord, I've already got one, it's one of the first appliances I had to buy, Bob insisted, he adores homemade french fries. His mother always used to make them, just in a wire basket in a cast-iron pot, but the idea of doing it that way scares the daylights out of me, so I got the electric thing. Can you imagine me sitting around watching Bob devour french fries? I'll weep."

"It seems people don't need stoves anymore, all they need are appliances," I said, and looked up past blenders and saw Warren watching me. And still he was just a guy, and I had to remind myself that he was the only guy I'd ever slept with, except David, that without him I might have gone insane in my apartment with my mirrors, that he had been important. My personality, I was learning, always somewhat disappeared into other people's, and always had, even alone all day writing in Thornhill, when I became my people I wrote. I had been David nearly forever, but briefly, superficially, I had been Warren. We looked at each other, the blenders between us reflecting each other opaquely.

"Twenty-two ninety-five," Kaykay said, making a note on her list. "Well, I'll tell Bob, but I think we'd better buy one at a real store. I guess that's it, there's nothing else I want here."

I bought my razor blades and we drove home. Grace was ironing blouses in the kitchen.

"What did you have to eat?" Kaykay said. "Tell us every single thing."

"Roast beef," Grace began, and Kaykay wailed, "I knew it! What else?" Grace said, "Let's see, mashed potatoes and lima beans and a salad—"

I said, "The hell with the salad. Did you have gravy?"

"Oh, of course, and Mom had made gingerbread for dessert."

"With whipped cream?"

"Well, with that Cool Whip stuff."

Kaykay said, "I bet she sent the gingerbread home with you."

"Yes, would you like some? I don't suppose there's much protein in it."

"Oh, God," Kaykay groaned, and took an orange out of the refrigerator.

It was later in the evening, after Kaykay and I had had our forlorn supper of salad and broccoli and tried not to ogle the chicken pie Grace ate, and we were watching *The Bill Cosby Show* with Bob who had come over bringing along a little snack for himself and Grace (a pint of fried clams and a pint of fried onion rings) when the phone rang.

"I'll get it," Grace said. Then she said in an odd tone, "Emily, it's for you. It's not your mother, it's a man's voice."

I put down my scotch slowly. Nobody except Lucy ever called me. I went to the counter and picked up the receiver. "Hello?"

"Hello, this is Warren."

He'd remembered that I couldn't identify telephone voices. "Oh," I said, not knowing what else to say.

"I was wondering if you'd like to come over and watch Glen Campbell at my place."

Glen Campbell's show had moved to Sunday nights.

For a split second I almost said yes, because of the same reason he'd invited me, sex, and then I said, "No, no, thank you, I guess I'll watch it here."

"Oh. Well."

"Good-bye."

I went back to the living room. Kaykay and Grace looked at me; Grace looked away again to the television, but Kaykay said, "It was that Warren, wasn't it?"

"Yes."

"Some nerve. What did he want?"

"A change of cunt," I said, and was stunned to see Grace blush red. Bob and Kaykay began laughing, and I picked up one of Kaykay's cigarettes and my scotch and went into the bedroom and got out my diary. I lay on my bed and smoked and sipped and read:

Wed., July 13, 1955. Carol's mother drove us to Stark's Dairy Bar at twenty of ten. It wasn't too busy, and we had fun. Nancy was taking "The Cow" apart, and took a strategic screw out of the nozzle. She plugged the normal hole with her finger and pulled down on the handle, just to see what would happen. Milk sprayed out of the hole where the screw was supposed to be, hitting Nancy square in the face. Rivulets dripped down the front of her uniform. Funny—Carol and Jeannine and I just about died. Then she tried to set off a whipped cream jet with the ice cream containers' carrying hook. Then we had a hell of a water fight with the hose we use for cleaning up—that is, Nancy and Jeannine did, but Jeannine grabbed me as a hostage and I got soaked.

During our break, Carol and I changed into our bathing suits and went to the beach. I fell asleep, and then Carol woke me up because there were some people from the Playhouse—*Guys and Dolls* cast—near us. They were singing, and seemed so relaxed. I wonder what it'd be like to work summer stock—going from place to place—but most of all, to be independent. They were comparatively kids—maybe five years older than me. I want to do new things and see new things—except for David. He's a permanent resident.

When we got back to Stark's, the thunderstorm which had begun to threaten broke loose. Was it fun!! Rain poured down in sheets and the wind was just right so that it came thru the screen to us. Everything blew all over the place, and the electricity went off, and so did the water. The frappe machines, the frappe cup washer, the scoop trench faucets, the freezers, the cabinets, the clock, all didn't work. Hurrah! Immediately we started eating. I managed to down a strawberry soda, a dish of vanilla ice cream with pineapple sauce, and a dish of frozen pudding ice cream. We sat on the cabinets, which we're not supposed to sit on, eating and reading. I read my W. Somerset Maugham's *Theatre*. I like it very much so far. He sure is fond of writing about affairs...*Up at the Villa, Christmas Holiday*, etc. The other kids read the confession magazines Jeannine brought the other day. In fact, Carol was so deep in a dramatic masterpiece entitled "Foolish Virgin" when the thunderstorm stopped and the electricity came on and customers began arriving again that she took the magazine home with her.

David picked me up at ten after six. He was hot and filthy from the gas station, so we went to the beach and went swimming, except we did more making out in the water than swimming. I got soundly splashed and ducked. It was so much fun. After he dives underwater his eyelashes get all stuck together and sort of starry. He has such long eyelashes!

Then he took me home, and Susan and Lucy and I had supper. A few of our peas were ready, so we had those, and our lettuce—Susan made the special dressing that Ma and Lucy make, out of tomato soup—and Lucy made cheese dreams. I ate in my uniform, and after my bath I put on my blue Bermudas and pink jersey, plus David's little gold football, of course of course.

At eight he picked me up. We drove downtown, parked the car, and entered the theater after Bob Hope in *The Seven Little Foys* had begun. It was pretty good. The second movie was *Return of the Creature*, a continuation of *The Creature from the Black Lagoon*. God, was it scary! Toward the end, there was a part where the hero was looking for the creature along the shore, and all of a sudden a hand reached out. The audience, as one, shrieked—including me, and I threw myself against David, burying my head on his shoulder. It was only the hand of the heroine. Up to that point, David and I had just been holding hands, but I guess then he figured that I needed a little more protection, so he put his arm around me. He laughed and laughed at my fright.

Afterward, we went to Joe's Drive-In and he had a chocolate frappe and I had a cheeseburger and Coke. I absolutely couldn't face any more ice cream.

Then we went to Bickford Park to go parking, but all the swings and stuff were up, as they hadn't been the times we parked there this spring, so we clambered out of the car, and I swang while David made like a gorilla on the trapeze, and then we both swang and investigated the swimming pool, and I sat down on the merry-go-round and David started pushing it and I nearly died of dizziness. We crossed the little bridge over the brook. Then we played on the seesaw; David weighs so much more than me that I was up in the air all the time. At last we returned to the car and finally settled down, after David had made several flattering remarks about my legs. And then awaaay we went! He got fresh again, but what the hell.

We came to at midnight and drove to my house. We just couldn't part, and when finally he walked me to the door he kept right on walking in and we found ourselves making out like mad on the living room couch. Lucy and Susan had gone to bed, thank God. David got overwhelmed by everything, and we nearly Went All the Way. Oh, I want to!!! He's so wonderful and I love him so much!!! But I made him stop, and he sat up and gathered me into his arms, and I tried to explain to him how it wasn't right, we couldn't. He was quiet for a while, and then he said, "I know, I know," and he said he was sorry. He asked, "We love each other, don't we?" "Yes," I said, and he continued, "Then that's all that matters, isn't it?" We talked in whispers, and everything was okay. He left at about one thirty, after lifting me off the threshold when kissing me. Devastating.

• • •

The office secretary's voice over the intercom said to the classroom, "We have received another bomb threat. Everybody is asked to leave the building in an orderly fashion."

Jesus H. Christ, I thought, and my kids were muttering the same. It was the third bomb scare in two weeks; it was no longer exciting.

"All right," I said, "you know the procedure." As they began to wander out of the room, I considered staying here and trying to find some way of letting them discover what "The Road Not Taken" was about, and then I looked out the windows. Friday afternoon, with a week of vacation ahead. A warm sunny April day, our first true spring day. I wouldn't even need my coat. So I followed the kids outdoors.

The buds on the trees were a pale-yellow-green mist. If I were in Thornhill on a day like this, after I finished my writing I would put on my bathing suit and go out back and sunbathe on the chaise longue, reading seed catalogs, deciding what we would plant this year in our gardens.

The house we rented in Thornhill was on a dead-end street on the outskirts of town. It was an old, decrepit house, but it had a big backyard. In the summer, a good part of the yard became David's garden. There was corn, his favorite vegetable, and there were radishes and tomatoes and lettuce and summer squash and carrots and cucumbers, and, after the agonizingly long wait of four years, asparagus, my favorite. And around the house were my flower beds, daffodils and narcissus and tulips in the springtime, and then nasturtiums and marigolds and zinnias and petunias, and the morning glories were a wondrous blue when we ate our summer breakfasts on the porch.

"Hey," Cliff Parker said, walking toward me. "Guess what's happened."

"They haven't found a real bomb!"

"Oh, hell, no, the cops aren't even here yet. It's this: Miss Higgins is going to retire."

"Who," I said, "is Miss Higgins?"

"Who is Miss Higgins? Who is Miss Higgins? Miss Higgins," he said, grinning at me, "is the head of the English Department at North Riverton High School. She has been the head of the English Department at North Riverton High School as long as anyone can remember. She was my teacher. She was my folks' teacher. She was, for all I know, my grandparents' teacher. That's who Miss Higgins is."

"And she is going to retire."

"I was beginning to think I'd have to drive up there some icy day and push her down the school steps. Not to kill her, you understand, just to break her hip. In hopes that an intimation of mortality might suggest to her it was time to hand in her red pencil."

"You'll apply for her job?" I asked, and all at once wondered what it would be like working here without him, without his easiness or his packets of Nabs and his entertaining chat in the teachers' room. I thought quickly over the other English teachers who might be promoted to his job if someone new wasn't brought in, and I couldn't imagine anything but madness resulting from working for them.

"I already have," he said. "Would you like a Pall Mall, to celebrate?" He lit them. "A friend of mine, the science teacher there, called me up last night to tell me the great news, so I called up the superintendent and asked if I could come for an interview, which is rather ridiculous since he's been the superintendent since I was in kindergarten, and he said sure, I can bring my transcripts and fill out the application when I get there. So I'm going up Monday."

"Oh," I said.

"Would you like to come along for the scenery?"

I stared at him. Then the police car, no siren, arrived, so I was able to turn away and watch the two policemen stroll leisurely into the school while I tried to think.

"I'm sorry," Cliff said. "I just wondered if you might like to see some of the north country again. We haven't got much time left to see it before it's a Levittown of A-frames."

Now the fire engine, also no siren, arrived.

"Well," I said, wildly trying to figure whether or not we'd have to go through Thornhill to get to North Riverton. I didn't even know if David and Ann were still there; most likely they had moved on to another town. But Thornhill itself would be there. And Monday was our wedding anniversary.

I took a deep drag of the cigarette, for courage, and asked, exposing my feelings, "Do you have to go through Thornhill?"

"Not if you don't want to."

And so I thought about the trip. When had I last been on a long trip? There were my job-hunting trips. And there was the time, about a year before the divorce, when David, restless, said we needed a change, and although we couldn't afford it we went to Boston; but that, from Plymouth on, had been a turnpike trip, with Howard Johnson stops and a night in a motel. I thought about seeing the Old Man of the Mountain again.

I said, "Could I bring along a picnic?"

Right here, with all the kids milling around the lawn, he touched my hair. "That'll be great. I'll buy some beer." He hesitated, and I suddenly knew he was going to ask me out tonight, but then he said, "I'll pick you up at eight Monday morning," and walked away.

I saw Grace standing alone watching us. I went over to her, and Kaykay emerged from a throng of teachers and said, "Honest to God, this is getting to be a bore. Mrs. LaBrecque says it was a kid's voice on the phone again, a girl's, and the bomb is supposed to go off at two o'clock."

We looked at our watches. It was two.

Kaykay said, "They ought to let us go home, the whole next hour will be nothing but a waste, vacation starting early. What were you and Curlytop having such a heart-to-heart about, adjective clauses?"

"He's going to North Riverton for an interview Monday and he invited me along for the ride."

"Are you going?"

"Yes."

"And Bob and I are going to Witherell Monday. Here it is again, the time of year when teachers play musical chairs with schools, and, Emily and Grace, you really ought to get into the game."

I said, "I've signed my contract." It had been so much simpler to do than job hunt.

Kaykay said, "You didn't sign it in blood, did you? You can resign; give them thirty days' notice. You, too, Grace."

"My folks—" Grace began, and Kaykay said, "As I tell you every year, they've got Wendy and Norma right in the same town, there's no need for you to stay, they'll be fine."

"Maybe," Grace said, and for the first time I heard the frightening bitterness in her voice. Kaykay and I glanced at each other; I realized Grace would be alone all day Monday at the apartment, while we were off on trips with men.

Kaykay said, "Let's stop at Lum's and have a beer after this damn day is finally over."

When the assistant principal came to the front door and announced that no bomb had been found and we should return to our classrooms, I walked back thinking of what I should make for a picnic. I hadn't fed a man since Warren. Kaykay and I had abandoned the no-protein phase after going crazy one evening and massacring a pound of Grace's ground chuck, so my diet was no problem, I'd just have to eat as tiny as possible. What were our lunches when David and I went on picnics along country roads and brooks in Thornhill? Tunafish sandwiches, potato chips. No, I thought as I told the kids to settle down and opened my book again to "The Road Not Taken." Something different from that. Potato salad, this time. Cold cuts. Cheese.

• • •

Cliff was a driver of back roads, in order, he said, to look his last on all things lovely before they were destroyed by turnpikes or housing developments. So we drove through towns with names like Center Barnstead and Gilmanton, past farms and woods, and then around Lake Winnipesaukee to Meredith, and on to the mountains.

His car was an old classic Volvo, a pale cream puff, and he obviously took tender care of it.

He hummed commercials and hymns, interchangeably, as we drove. All at once I felt very happy. I was going on a journey with someone I enjoyed, and we would have a picnic. And although we were leaving spring behind the farther north we drove, and although this feeling was rather foolish, perhaps, at my advanced age, I felt also like springtime. Rebirth? I looked down at my yellow jersey, short green culotte, display of nylon-encased legs, and little yellow shoes, and realized that at least I *looked* like springtime, and I looked quite nice.

I didn't remember Grace, home alone, until we reached Plymouth.

"Grace went to school here," I said. "Damn it all," I added, thinking out loud, "there's absolutely no reason for a girl to be plain these days, I don't know why Kaykay and I don't hog-tie her and do something about her hair and get her some way-out clothes, like in those movies you used to see, the plain-Jane secretary lets down her hair and takes off her glasses, and her boss says, 'Good heavens, is it—it can't be—can it be—is it you, Miss Bigelow?' and instantaneously marries her."

Cliff was laughing. "Why don't you?"

"How can we? All we can do is hint. Kaykay got her to go see about contact lenses a couple of years ago, saying how everyone says they're so convenient and comfortable and all that, but Grace found out she can't wear them, her eyes aren't teary enough or some damn thing."

Then we were in the White Mountains. The road was so familiar. The motels, the smelly polluted river, the place that had the trained bears I grieved for every time we drove past. The Indian Head profile of rock far above us impassively ignored the motel resort, the campground, the trading post, and the animal farm below it.

And then there was nothing but mountains. The road rose higher and higher through Franconia Notch, and I leaned out the window to try to see the tops of the mountains, knowing that I couldn't, and I couldn't.

Cliff said, "I always forget how hypnotizing these mountains are, I always want to drive straight at them."

"Please don't."

He laughed, but his knuckles were white on the steering wheel. David, too, had found it difficult to drive this road.

A small sign announced the Old Man of the Mountain. I crouched down in the seat so I could see higher out Cliff's window, and when the moment came I saw the Old Man beautifully clearly, his rock profile solemn against the sky.

I heard myself saying, "School would get too much for David every once in a while, and we would drive down here and look at the Old Man, and everything would be all right." Then I said quickly, to cover up, "Are they really going to put a turnpike through here?"

"Well, they've been told not to, so we're safe for a time. What about Thornhill? I can take back roads again."

We passed the ski area, and involuntarily I said, "We used to go skiing there. We couldn't've afforded it, except we knew the guy who took tickets and he let us in free." I slipped Cliff's pack of Pall Malls out of his pocket and lit one.

He hummed, "We gather together to ask the Lord's blessing, He chastens and hastens His will to make known."

"Not appropriate," I said. I sang, "The bear went over the mountain, the bear went over the mountain."

"I was brought up Methodist, Emily, and unfortunately I know a great many hymns."

The Thornhill question still awaited an answer. The high gray road began its swoop into the valley, and the white safety posts whipped past. I said, "I think I would like to see Thornhill again."

"You sure?"

"No. Yes."

Foothills rushed up at us, carrying past us a house of tar paper and a cow, cellar holes and forgotten orchards, and then there were A-frames.

"Oh, no," I said. "There's more of them."

He said, "I think they must multiply like amoebae," and braked to a stop at the corner by the lumber mill. We turned and drove down Main Street.

I looked at the grocery store where I had bought our food with David's money, the five-and-ten where I bought manila envelopes to mail away my stories, the laundromat where I washed our clothes, the drugstore where I bought my Pills.

Cliff suddenly made fast conversation. "If this is your first year teaching, what did you do all the time you lived here?"

"Wrote stuff that nobody bought. There's the library, what a silly little one it is, it's only open about two minutes a week. I read my way straight through it, murder mysteries, love stories, books on gardening, biographies of Napoleon, even the town history. The woman who was the librarian must be as old as your Miss Higgins, but by God she remembered everyone and we didn't even need library cards," I said, and when I'd finished I had stopped shaking and I could look up at the old brick school on the hill above the river.

"You okay?" he asked.

"Don't worry," I said, smiling at him, "I can't cry, I'd ruin my eye makeup."

But was David still here, was David still here? And was my ghost still here for him, haunting these stores, haunting this town, did he sometimes forget and think I would be waiting for him in that shabby house on that dead-end street, did he drive home to me and our beers and our suppers and our evenings of television and our bed?

There was the street. I didn't say anything, and we drove past.

Cliff said, "It's a nice town."

"Yes. I liked it." I took another cigarette from him. "Are they considering anyone else in the department for head?"

"I doubt it. The school is so small, like Thornhill, that there're only two other English teachers, and Miss Higgins is such a holy terror there's always a turnover, nobody wants to stay and work with her. The other two are always kids fresh out of Plymouth or Brompton, they teach a year with her and then flee."

"So you've got it made, with your experience."

"Knock on wood."

We drove past the big old gray tavern with its six chimneys, once a stagecoach stop, now nothing, rotting silently. We drove along the river where in the summer you saw red-winged blackbirds. There were fields and pastures and farmhouses, and new little houses in hostile colors, turquoise and pink, and there were trailers.

WELCOME TO NORTH RIVERTON, the small sign said. ESTABLISHED 1763.

The school was an old brick one near the common. We parked in front of it just as the clock in the town hall struck eleven.

"You sure you don't mind waiting?" he said. "You could get some coffee or something over there in the drugstore."

"No, I'm fine," I said, unbuckling my seat belt and taking my paperback Nero Wolfe out of my pocketbook. I looked at him, and suddenly he leaned down, and we kissed. I said, "Good luck."

But instead of reading, I watched the kids, also on vacation this week, hanging around in front of the few stores. There was the Riverton Inn, white with a wide porch. A dog ran across the common, sniffed at the statue of a soldier (Civil War? World War I? I couldn't tell from here), and ran on.

No shopping plazas, no Miracle Mile. But soon, I supposed, there would be, complete with self-service liquor store.

And just as I thought I'd succeeded in thinking of this and not of Thornhill, out of nowhere crashed the memory: awakening early in the mornings when David was still asleep, his head on my shoulder, his breathing warming my skin. I would lie there and love his breathing and wonder what I'd do if it ever stopped.

Cliff came out of the school an hour later.

"How'd it go?" I asked, closing my book as he got in the car.

He was grinning, and he kissed me again and said, "I signed the contract."

My stomach plunged with fear. "Hey, great," I said.

He took off his sport jacket and tossed it into the back seat and took off his tie. "The poor guy was kind of flabbergasted when he saw the beard, but then he must've remembered what an honest American boy I used to be, and he rallied." He started the car. "Now, look, I ought to go see my folks, since I'm here, but if we show up at lunchtime my mother will start racing around the kitchen and insist on feeding us more food than you've ever seen in your life, so why don't we go have our picnic now and we can truthfully say we've already eaten."

"Fine with me."

He drove along the street and parked again. "I'll just run into Downing's and get the beer. Budweiser okay?"

"Fine."

I watched him go into the grocery store and sat numbly staring at the signs in its window—PREMIUM BACON 79¢ LB., CUKES 4 FOR 39¢, HOMEMADE GRINDERS 49¢—until he came out carrying a six-pack.

We drove north out of town and then down back roads through woods, past farms. The roads became dirt, became narrower, and at last he stopped the car.

"We have to walk from here," he said, picking up the picnic basket I'd bought Saturday. "Is it too chilly, do you want your coat?"

"I'm fine," I said. "Let me carry something."

He gave me the blanket and we started walking down the path.

"Oh, my God," he said.

There was an A-frame regarding us through the trees with its big triangular eye.

"Damn it all, damn it all," he said.

"I'm sorry."

"I should've expected it, that bastard McLaughlin would sell anything to anybody. But his land ends here; we're safe from any more."

We walked along the path. The trees hadn't yet begun to bud, and the sun through the naked branches made dancing crisscross shadows everywhere. I took a deep breath of the clear warm breeze.

Then we left the path, and I followed him through the trees down a hill to a brook.

"Your stockings," he said. "I didn't think."

"They're quite intact," I said, spreading the blanket. "Wonders of modern science."

We sat down and watched the brook swirl around rocks.

I said, "You used to fish here."

"I damn near lived here," he said, and popped open a couple of beers, handed one to me, and put the tabs neatly into the picnic basket. "Hey," he said, investigating its contents, "this looks good."

I started to reach in to take things out, and he said, "As does this," and his hand was on my thigh and we were kissing. My stomach growled. We laughed.

So we ate, and watched the brook, and after our second beers we both went off on private journeys into the woods. We smoked his cigarettes, careful of ashes and butts. He talked about his fishing here and camping out overnight, and he always seemed on the verge of saying something else, yet he didn't.

It was, I realized, a good way to spend what would have been our eleventh anniversary; in fact, David and I had picnicked on anniversaries during our earlier years when we couldn't afford to go out to dinner. One time we'd made love in the crushed grass of a deer's bed.

On Ma and Pop's anniversaries, Ma's diary had told me:

• • •

Wed., April 3, 1907. Our first anniversary. Dr. thinks baby not getting enough to eat, so began feeding her partly on bottle with Holt's Formula No. One. Chester gave me Ferruzzi's Madonna and I gave him a modern Madonna.

Fri., April 3, 1908. Had Jacksons and Burnhams to dinner. Chester gave me an Indian Tree platter and I gave him a card table.

Sat., April 3, 1909. Cold and snowy. Had bad cold and didn't go out. Lucy stole two gumdrops and threw up in P.M.

• • •

I remembered their fiftieth anniversary and the big party Lucy had engineered in her efficient way, a surprise party at Ma and Pop's house. Lucy had sent invitations to their hundreds of friends, and she and Susan and I had made acres of hors d'oeuvres, packed them, somehow got them all into the car, and drove down to Lexington. The friends arriving, Ma weeping, the rooms growing more and more crowded with old people laughing and drinking, while Susan and I, embarrassed teenagers, stood about awkwardly and watched.

Cliff slid his hand along my leg. "I've been interested in doing this ever since I saw you at that first teachers' meeting."

"If you had, it'd've sent our colleagues into a tizzy."

"You look like a flower."

"It's springtime."

He said, "Let's pick up my camping gear at my folks' house and spend the night here. I'll catch you trout for supper. I'll catch you trout for breakfast. I cook trout very well."

"The season isn't open yet."

"That's never stopped me."

I pressed his hand between my thighs, but although camping here seemed a wonderful idea, I said, "No. No, we'd better go back," and began putting our paper plates and napkins into the basket. Cock teaser, I accused myself.

I'd thought we would drive back into town, but we continued on the dirt road through woods and past a pasture, and then Cliff turned at a mailbox that said PARKER and we drove up to a long white farmhouse and a big gray barn.

"Good heavens," I said.

"It's my grandparents', really. When my father and mother got married they built a house on the land down the road.

During the Depression. Then when my grandparents died we moved back here and rented the other house. This hasn't really been a farm since my grandfather died. My father worked at the shoe factory, he just retired, so we mostly only had chickens and rabbits and a couple of pigs. I had a horse for a while."

"It's a beautiful place."

"Well, they've managed to keep it up, and they haven't sold any land. Not like McLaughlin, the bastard. Brace yourself, my mother'll go wild. Only child, that's me."

We got out of the car. The side door of the house opened and a buxom woman in a housedress and apron cried, "Cliff! What on earth!"

"Hi there, Mother," he said, and she said, "That awful beard," and embraced him. "You're still too thin!" she said. "It's your vacation, isn't it? I *wondered* if you'd be coming up." Then she noticed me and smiled a delighted smile. "Why, Cliff. Who's this?"

"This is Emily Bean," he said, taking my hand and drawing me forward. "She teaches English with me."

I said, "How do you do," and we smiled at each other, and she said, "Come in, come in. Have you eaten?"

"Oh, yes," Cliff said, "we just ate."

"How about some coffee and some pie? I made a lemon meringue pie this morning."

Cliff looked helplessly at me, and we went into the sunny kitchen. The linoleum was worn but shiny with floor wax. In the windows there were nearly as many plants as in Susan's kitchen windows. It was the kitchen I'd always wanted, old sink and cupboards, humming refrigerator, black iron stove, red-oilcloth-covered table, the warm smell of cooking. A kitchen from my early childhood, Lucy's kitchen, Ma's kitchen, before newer refrigerators and stoves were bought.

Mrs. Parker said, "You go on into the living room and I'll bring the coffee—"

"Now, Mother," Cliff said, and sat down at the kitchen table. "Where's Dad?"

She didn't answer immediately, bustling more than necessary with coffeepot and cups. Then she said, "He's taking a nap, I'll go call him."

The cups and saucers and plates were exactly the same kind Ma had used for everyday, a set of different colors, pink and blue and green and yellow, always chipped and mismatched.

Cliff paused in offering me a cigarette. "Dad doesn't take naps. Does he?"

"He's started to lately. It does him good," she said defensively, and poured our coffee.

"Don't wake him then."

"What do you think he'd do if I let him sleep through your visit?" she asked, and next asked the question all mothers ask. "How long can you stay?"

"We ought to be heading back."

"I'll go call him," she repeated, cutting the pie and setting pieces on our plates. The meringue was an inch thick.

When she left the kitchen, Cliff said, "A nap. Good God, a nap." He ground out his cigarette in the glass ashtray and stabbed his fork into his pie.

"It's glorious pie," I said.

"Yes, she's known for her pies."

I said, "Have they heard about Miss Higgins?"

"She'd've mentioned it if they had."

"Sometimes I take a nap when I get home from school."

"I guess I do, sometimes," he said.

Mrs. Parker returned. "He's coming down. Do you live in Millbridge, Emily?"

"In Hull," I said, "with a couple of other girls." Girls? I amended, "They teach at Millbridge, too."

Cliff said, "Great pie, Mother. As always."

I said, "It certainly is."

We didn't distract her. She said, "Are you from Hull?"

"No, from Saundersborough, I grew up in Saundersborough."

"That's a nice place. All those lovely old houses. Is this your first year at Millbridge?"

"Yes," I said, and just when I knew she was going to ask me where else I'd taught, Mr. Parker came in. His hair was a preview of what Cliff's would be, as curly and white as the meringue on the pie. He wore no beard, so I could see the deep cleft in his chin, and I wondered if Cliff also had one.

"Well, Cliff," he said, and Cliff stood up and they self-consciously shook hands.

"This is Emily Bean," Cliff said.

We said hello, and Mr. Parker's eyes, blue like Cliff's, twinkled at me. He pulled up a chair and sat down at the table.

Mrs. Parker poured him coffee and asked, "More pie, Cliff? Emily?"

"Thank you, no," we said.

Mr. Parker said, "What brings you up here?"

"A job," Cliff said, and instantly they were alert. He said, "Miss Higgins is going to retire."

Mrs. Parker sat down abruptly in the rocking chair by the stove.

Mr. Parker said, "Judas Priest." Then he said, "I beg your pardon, Emily."

"Did you see Matthew?" Mrs. Parker cried. "Oh, no, you didn't go to see Matthew with that beard, did you?"

Cliff said, "As a matter of fact, I did, and he offered me the job. I signed the contract."

"Oh, Cliff!" she said, and rushed over to him and hugged him. Mr. Parker beamed at us.

Cliff said, "Of course, the school board has to okay it—"

"The school board!" Mrs. Parker said, laughing and sniffling, fishing a Kleenex out of the bosom of her dress.

Mr. Parker picked up the pipe and tobacco pouch on the table. "I don't think the school board will be any problem," he said, tamping tobacco.

"No," Cliff said, "neither do I," and they laughed. "Nepotism," he explained to me. "My uncle's on the school board."

Mrs. Parker said, "When will you be coming back, when does Millbridge let out in June?" I knew her head was busy with the cleaning of his room somewhere upstairs, the dusting and polishing and washing she would do. I saw her suddenly remember the question of me, and I saw her excitement mount and realized that this was what she wanted most, Cliff to be married. I wondered, as I'd always wondered, why he hadn't.

She said, "Would you like more coffee, Emily? More pie?"

"More coffee would be great, but I'd still better restrain myself about the pie."

She poured coffee. "You wouldn't by any chance be up here for an interview as well?"

"Oh, no, I'm just along for the ride."

"Can't you two stay for supper? It's only the beans left over from Saturday, and yesterday's roast, but there's time to make some of those bran rolls you love, Cliff—"

Cliff, giving me a cigarette, said, "We really ought to be getting back, Mother."

Mr. Parker looked at Mrs. Parker, and there was a brief discreet silence. Did they suppose we were hurriedly returning to a love nest?

Cliff said, "Matthew did quite well by me, you'll see it in your taxes. He asked what I wanted, and I said I was making ten thousand five hundred and forty now, and he said the step I'd be on here was nine thousand eight hundred and sixty, and I said let's have a round number like ten thousand, and he went along with it. God only knows what he got away with paying poor Miss Higgins all these years."

"My goodness, ten thousand dollars," Mrs. Parker said admiringly, taking away our plates. "Isn't that nice."

I said, "Let me help you wash up."

"No, no, it'll be no trouble at all. Look," she said, and for the first time I noticed the dishwasher. "Cliff and his father gave it to me last Christmas. When I was out in the kitchen making the eggnog, they sneaked it into the living room, they'd hidden it in the barn. They put it under the Christmas tree—well, beside it, you know—and it had a big red ribbon on it."

"Aforementioned uncle," Cliff said to me, "has a hardware and appliance store. Very handy."

Mrs. Parker said, "I never ever thought I'd want one, and now I don't know how I managed without it. The Christmases I got my washing machine and my dryer, I tried to be pleased but I couldn't see any reason to have a new washing machine, and as for a dryer, what was wrong with sunshine? I've been using sunshine all my life. But of course I changed my mind. And now they keep wanting to get me a new stove, and I just know I wouldn't like a new one, I just know it. And a refrigerator. Why on earth should I want a new refrigerator when this one is still working fine?"

"No defrosting," Cliff began, looked at me, and grinned. "Wonders of modern science," he said, and we had our secret joke about my nylons.

"Well, I don't know," Mrs. Parker said. "Maybe. It'd be awfully easy, wouldn't it? I hear those new stoves actually clean themselves."

We stubbed out our cigarettes, and Cliff pushed back his chair and stood up.

"Now," Mrs. Parker said, ripping Saran Wrap, "you take the rest of the pie with you, you can bring back the pie plate next time you come home."

Again Cliff looked at me helplessly. He said, "Thank you, Mother. I'll drop you a card to let you know when I'll be up."

We all went outdoors.

"What a nice day," Mrs. Parker said.

Mr. Parker said, "There'll be another snowstorm."

"You always say that!" she said.

"There usually is," he said, and I remembered that in Thornhill there usually was.

Mrs. Parker kissed Cliff, and he and his father shook hands once more.

I said, "It was very good to meet you."

"Come again soon," they said, and Mrs. Parker added, "Why don't you see if you can't make him shave off that awful beard, Emily?"

Cliff was laughing as we drove down the dirt road.

We took another way home, through Bethlehem and Twin Mountain, and through Crawford Notch. At first we mostly looked at the mountains, and then we began talking about Ethan Allen Crawford's adventures here, and as we neared Cate we talked about Millbridge and our principal, who had been a gym teacher and whom, as I'd suspected and now learned, Cliff despised.

"He can't even get his clichés right," Cliff said. "Remember the last teachers' meeting, he said, 'If on this side you had a hole and you stuck your hand in it'? Remarkable."

We drove along Cate's coy main street.

I said, "My sister lives here."

"Does she? Do you want to stop?"

"I guess not, thanks."

From Cate he drove the back roads I myself had discovered on my second trip to Susan's, and we went through little villages of old white houses.

And then we were in Hull. I wanted it to be this morning all over again, with the trip ahead of us.

He said, "How about a drink, to celebrate the job? This place is a nightmare and the drinks are terrible, but they're the best in town."

It was the Hampshire Motel. I walked into the baronial cocktail lounge with Cliff instead of Warren.

"What would you like?" he asked when we'd sat down at one of the little candlelit tables.

"A martini, please."

The waitress was new, the room dark. She said, "I'm sorry, miss, but do you have any identification?"

"Oh," I said, "how absolutely marvelous!" and hauled forth my billfold and got out my driver's license, which showed I'd turned thirty-one last week.

"For heaven's sake," she said, and went off to the bar.

Cliff said, "Did she think I was robbing the cradle?"

I laughed, and then, as he reached toward the bowl of potato chips, I thought, my God, his hands are like David's. They were very square hands, with square flat nails. I saw David's hands moving about his desk in the evenings when he prepared to correct papers; he and I were neat, a trait intensified by our years together, but he was even neater with his desk than I was with mine. His was a battered roll-top he had discovered in the loft of a second-hand store, and in the evenings his hands tidied the contents of pigeonholes, arranged a stack of books according to size, nudged the rank book until its left side matched the right side of the blotter, and chose two red pencils and put them with the fountain pen, points away from him, beside the pile of papers. Once I had said, watching him straighten everything again after he'd finished work, "It must be superstition. If you don't keep the dictionary lined up beside the Elmer's Glue-All, you'll forget to pay the income tax and we'll go to jail." "Wise guy," he had said.

Now Cliff was holding the candle aloft and peering around.

I said, "Let me guess. You're looking for an honest man."

"I'm looking for our drinks."

They came, so he held the candle forward to me and I lit a cigarette off the flame. We drank, and he said, "I gather you haven't applied for a job at another school."

"No. I signed my contract."

After a silence, he said, "People aren't clawing at each other in a desperate rush to teach at schools like North Riverton, but they ought to be, because such schools aren't going to exist much longer. North Riverton has been talking for years about a regional high school, consolidated with towns around it like Thornhill, and someday it will happen and I'll have to go along with it, but until then I'll have this last chance to teach at a small high school."

What was he explaining?

He grinned and said, "The classrooms still smell of manure, just as they always did."

And just as David's classroom in Thornhill had, the few times I'd visited it. The dark old classroom, the faint warm smell of manure, the blackboards that were black, not modern green, David's desk as neat as at home, and nothing on the walls, because David hated bulletin boards, except a brownish painting of Anne Hathaway's cottage, and the old clock which clicked and jerked each minute forth.

I realized I'd eaten my olive and was chewing on the plastic toothpick. Back then, I had never dreamed I too would have a classroom. Pale-blue cinder-block.

Cliff was studying me. He seemed to hesitate. "Well," he said, and changed the subject, asking obliquely, "it must be difficult, writing while you're teaching and taking that course."

"I'm not writing."

He was the first English teacher, besides David, I'd ever met who didn't say that he himself would write if he had the time. Even I had said it to Warren. Cliff said, "How about going out to dinner tonight?"

No. I was getting too involved. "I'd love to," I said, "only I've got to do homework, I have my class tomorrow night. I'm sorry."

But as we drove along the Miracle Mile he said, "What about the day after tomorrow? We could go to the beach or something and have dinner at the Seaside or someplace."

He gave me time to try to think of an excuse. He parked in front of my building and reached into the back seat for the picnic basket. "That pie," he said. "I'll gain ten pounds if I even look at it. Would you like it?"

"No, I'd gain twenty. But Grace wouldn't, if you really want to get rid of it."

"I sure do," he said, and put it in the basket. He looked at me. I couldn't think of an excuse.

"It's vacation," he said, and suddenly his arms were around me and he kissed me very thoroughly.

"Okay," I said, laughing. "Okay, let's go to the beach." I touched his beard. "I don't agree with your mother. I like it. It's sexy."

"Aha," he said.

When I went into the apartment I called, "Hi, I'm back," and put the pie in the refrigerator, the plastic containers and forks in the sink, the aluminum foil and paper plates and napkins in the wastebasket. Pollution, I thought guiltily. Pollution and habit; I should have used regular plates and bowls and silverware, cloth napkins and waxed paper, to help out Mother Nature a tiny bit. "Anybody home?" I called.

The toilet flushed. Grace came slowly into the living room. She was drunk. I had never seen her drunk.

She asked, "Did you have a good time?"

"In ways," I said, wondering if I should offer her coffee, or something more to drink so she'd pass out. She solved this by pouring herself a scotch.

"Busy busy day," she said. "I corrected papers this morning. I watched *The Galloping Gourmet*, and I had two beet sandwiches. I went to Norma's this afternoon and heard all about her kids and the ceramics class. She gave us that cream pitcher, she made it."

The cream pitcher stood on the counter. It was a ceramic cow. Grace tilted it by its tail, and it vomited milk.

She said, "Then I came home and had about ten drinks."

I sponged the milk off the counter. "Kaykay's not back from Witherell yet?"

"She'll be spending the night at Bob's. Vacation time."

I said, "There's some lemon meringue pie in the fridge."

"From where?"

"Cliff's mother. She's known for her pies."

Grace began to cry. Her face red and ugly, her sobs harsh, she stood there holding her glass and crying, and then she dropped the glass and it smashed on the tile floor, and she ran staggeringly into the bathroom.

I stood and listened to her retching between sobs. I got the broom and swept up glass, got the sponge and mopped up scotch.

Grace was quiet. I started toward the bathroom, and paused, and went back to the phone and looked for Bob's number in the phone book. I dialed, but nobody answered.

Grace came into the living room again. She'd brushed her hair and put on lipstick, and she smelled of mouthwash. She said, "Norma says the new Chinese restaurant downtown is very good. Why don't we have supper there?"

• • •

The sea was blue-green. The late afternoon was sunny and windy.

"Kite-flying weather," Cliff said, pointing toward the sky of kites and seagulls, "let's go watch," and he drove into the parking lot of the state beach. You didn't have to pay until summer.

He got out of the car and opened my door and I got out, reluctantly. Kites were David. He built them himself, and on spring afternoons, after school, he would fly them in our backyard. He'd constructed a reel out of a bicycle wheel to manipulate them, and sometimes kids would wander into the yard and watch their mad English teacher fly his kites.

The kite flyers here seemed to be mostly UNH kids, shouting and laughing, their high soaring kites suddenly plummeting into the waves.

I said, "I wonder how cold the water is."

"Freezing, I guarantee."

"Let's find out," I said, taking off my sandals, and all at once it was all right, I was running and laughing and he was chasing me across the sand down to the waves. I ran in up to my ankles. "Oh, my God, you're right, oh, my God," I shrieked, hopping up and down until the wave slid back, sucking sand from beneath my feet the way I always loved it to when I was little. Cliff had left his shoes and socks somewhere, and now he rolled up the bottoms of his pants and came after me as the next wave broke, and he chased me along through the surf toward the jetty of black rocks. I turned and shouted, "I'll win, you smoke more than I do!" and he shouted, "Look out!" and I felt twine graze the top of my head, and David said, "Emily."

I was so shocked I said quite naturally, "Where's your bicycle wheel?"

His fair hair was longer now, like everyone's. His shirt was one I'd never seen, one I'd never washed and ironed, and so were his corduroy pants.

But he was still David, more familiar to me than myself.

He said, "I'm trying this out," and I saw he had a small red plastic hand reel. I looked up at his kite in the sky. It was a black and yellow butterfly of plastic. And then I noticed Ann, sitting on a rock watching us. She was pregnant.

Proof. Proof of what I could never believe, David's sleeping with someone other than me.

Cliff came up. "You nearly got decapitated, you idiot," he said, and ruffled my hair. "I apologize," he said to David, and took my hand, seemed to sense something, and let go.

I said, "Cliff Parker. David Lewis. Where are you teaching?"

"Pleasantfield."

Which was a town south of here. So he had left the north country too, and he had been near me all along.

He said, "What are you doing?"

"Teaching at Millbridge."

Cliff walked away toward the rocks and began to climb them.

We stood together and looked up at his kite. The sun went behind the clouds but still shone on the Isles of Shoals, the white lighthouse translucent.

I realized I was trembling from head to foot.

David said, "Are you married to him?"

"No."

We watched the kite jerk and tug way out over the waves.

I wanted to touch him, I wanted him to put his arms around me, I wanted to kiss him.

I said, "You're joining in the population explosion."

"Yes."

It must be Ann's idea, I told myself. He had never wanted a baby before.

A boy and girl in commercially streak-faded blue Levi's shouted as the Frisbee they were playing with swooped into the ocean. The girl kicked off her loafers and went in after it; she splashed past us and I automatically moved nearer to David and then I remembered I couldn't.

Would he still smell the same, the David smell of clean skin and clean clothes?

He said, "Are you okay for money?"

"Yes. I'm making six thousand," I said, and was surprised to hear a note of pride in my voice, as in the Morning Man's.

"Pay scales certainly are higher down here," David said.

I said, "I drove through Thornhill the day before yesterday."

"I haven't been back. What's it like?"

"More A-frames."

"How's Lucy?"

"Fine," I said. "How're your folks?"

"Same as ever. Is Lucy still teaching this year?"

"Lord, yes, she's going strong. And she's signed up to teach remedial reading to junior high kids at the summer session, and you know how she is, she thought she ought to brush up, so she's taking another remedial reading course at Plymouth this summer as well. Busman's holiday."

He laughed.

Oh, David. Oh, David.

The kite danced in the sky.

I said, "Remember how I used to recite while you were kite flying, 'O by the by has anybody seen little you-i who stood on a green hill and threw his wish at blue'?"

Ann walked toward us. She was tall enough to carry her pregnancy well. She wore a ruffly white maternity blouse over pink slacks, and her brown hair was braided into pigtails tied with ribbons, one white and one pink. I thought suddenly of what I was wearing, a new gold shift that was so short it was practically a long jersey, and I was glad of it and glad that I'd started my tan.

"Hello, Emily," she said. "I'm going back to the car, David. My legs hurt."

I imagined with fierce joy varicose veins erupting purple through those legs that, instead of mine, could hold him tight.

But as she walked away he said, "I'll be along in a minute," and the time was running out.

I said, "Remember when Susan and John were at UNH and Lucy gave them the money to rent Ma's camp for a week before they had to start their summer jobs, and we came down from Thornhill for the weekend, and that Saturday we lugged six-packs out on the jetty and you and John had a kite-flying contest and we all drank beer and it's a wonder we didn't fall in the ocean we were so drunk."

"The kites themselves finally fell, as I recall."

"Then we went back to the camp and cooked hamburgers on the barbecue grill."

"I never ate so many hamburgers in my life."

We looked at each other, and then David looked up at the kite and began to reel it in.

"How's the writing?" he asked.

"I haven't done any."

He turned to me. "Emily. For God's sake. You once said that the only important thing is writing."

What I had said was the only important thing besides David was writing.

The kite made a wild dive and David turned back to his reeling in.

He said, "Do you like your job?"

"Not particularly."

"Does he teach in Millbridge, too?"

"Yes, he's the head of the English Department."

"You live in Millbridge?"

"No, in Hull, in an apartment with a couple of girls." If I gave him my address, would he come to see me? How long could pregnant women be screwed? Was Ann out of commission now, was he horny? Could this be a way I could see him again?

"Oh, damn," he said as the kite dropped into the ocean. "Well, it's plastic, it'll survive," and he reeled it in.

He stood holding it. We looked at each other.

He said, "Have you been all right?"

Oh, David. I love you.

Then I realized I'd said this aloud. I reached out and touched the pelt of blond hairs on his wrist. I was trembling, I was crying.

"Emily. Jesus Christ. Emily."

Hold me, please hold me.

He said, "Look, if you ever need anything, money or anything, you can call me at the school." He walked quickly away across the sand.

The waves were black waves crashing in on me, and I felt myself falling.

"Emily," Cliff's voice said. His arm was around my shoulders, and I sat up. Then I put my face against his chest and wept.

"It's okay," he said. "It's okay."

When I could speak, I said, "I left my pocketbook in the car, I haven't got a Kleenex."

He gave me his handkerchief and I blew my nose.

"Sorry," I said. "I've only done that twice before in my life." The first was the time when David, traveling to a class one evening a week in Plymouth, had got caught by a snowstorm and had telephoned to say he couldn't make it home and he would have to spend the night in Plymouth. I had put the phone down, and with the thought of the night ahead without him, the first night alone since we were married, the waves of blackness came. I didn't fall; I went to the sofa and lay down for a long time. Then I got drunk so I could sleep.

The other time was the evening he said, "There's something we've got to talk over," and I knew what it was, I had known for months but I wouldn't allow it into my mind, I'd become adept at blanking it out until it was only brief sick sweaty moments each day. And as David talked, his voice strange and rough and tormented, his words "Ann Turner" and "divorce," the words crashing in like waves, for one last time I blanked out the knowledge that we were dead, the world was dead, and the blackness engulfed me.

Cliff said, "Do you want to go home?"

"No. I want a drink."

I stood up and began brushing sand off me.

"May I help?" he said, and smiled tentatively at me, and I smiled back, and he helped brush. My bottom seemed to need a lot of brushing.

We found my sandals and his shoes and socks and sat on the wall and brushed off our feet and put them on. Then we went back to the parking lot where a group of UNH kids were trying to patch up a kite, asking each other, "Has anybody got any scotch tape?"

As we drove away to the Seaside Restaurant I saw only one kite still flying, a Mickey Mouse kite.

In the Lobster Buoy Lounge of lobster buoys and fishnets and starfish and clamshells, we sat down on one of the red-cushioned benches behind a little table and we both ordered martinis. When I took a cigarette, my hands still trembled violently. Cliff noticed and started talking about the way he planned to organize the English curriculum at North Riverton. I didn't listen, but his voice, and the cigarette and martini, began to soothe. My hands grew steadier.

But David. My David.

Cliff said, "Are you hungry?"

"I'm always hungry."

"Would you like another drink and we'll go out to the restaurant?"

At the next table a woman said, "New Hampshire Sweepstakes. Sweepstakes," she repeated. "I can't say that word since I had this tooth filed off."

I said, "Have you got any booze at your place?"

"Some scotch. Some rum. Some gin and vermouth."

"And I've got a gorgeous steak at mine," I said. "Why don't we go pick it up and I'll cook it at your house. I've got salad stuff, too."

He regarded me over his glass.

At the bar, somebody was saying, "—the drummer named Thumper, remember the time he fell in his drum?"

I said, "I cook a good steak."

"If that potato salad was any indication, you cook everything well."

"Yes. Except poached eggs, I've never mastered poaching an egg without one of those little egg poachers."

He drained his glass, looked at me again, and said, "Sounds like a fine idea."

So we drove back to Hull. Cliff hummed commercials. When I went into my apartment, Grace was eating a TV dinner and watching the news.

I said, "May I take the steak and some salad things? I'll reimburse everyone."

"Sure, go right ahead."

I took them out of the refrigerator and put them in a paper bag. Then I went into the bedroom and got a pair of underpants, went into the bathroom and got my toothbrush, and put these in my pocketbook.

I said, "We're cooking dinner at Cliff's place. I don't know when I'll be back. Where's Kaykay?"

"At Bob's."

"Oh," I said, and paused on my way out.

"Have fun," she said.

We drove through downtown and along residential streets.

"Hey," I said. "I used to live near here, on Brewster Street."

"I know."

"You know?"

"I used to see your car parked there. You were going out with the Morning Man."

The forsythia in front of the old white houses had begun to bloom springtime yellow.

He drove into the driveway of an enormous white house with porches and black shutters.

"I've noticed this one," I said. "It's a beauty."

"It's chopped up now into six apartments, but, yes, it's still a beauty."

We walked along a brick walk between yellow forsythia bushes and went up the steps to a side porch where old wicker furniture awaited summer. He unlocked the door.

Cliff, like Grace, had made a home. There was a fireplace in the living room, and a deep sofa and chairs, and the rug and the wall of books glowed with colors.

"Wow," I said, looking around. There was a spray of forsythia in an earthenware jug.

He said, "I had forsythia in March. You cut off some branches and pound the ends with a hammer, stick them in water, and they'll bloom."

"Is it called forcing?" I said, following him into the kitchen. I put the steak and lettuce and tomatoes in the refrigerator while he opened the high wooden cupboards.

"Martini?" he asked.

"Fine."

It was a big kitchen, painted apple-green. I tried to imagine his hanging the white Cape Cod curtains. David hung our curtains, of course, but that had been for me, not for himself. The kitchen table and chairs were like Cliff's folks', farmhouse drop-leaf table, slat-backed chairs. The table wasn't covered with oilcloth, however; instead, on it lay one place mat.

He stirred the martinis in a glass pitcher. "Fringe benefits," he said, holding up the glass rod. "When I broke my last one, the chemistry teacher made me this."

I laughed, he poured, and we carried our glasses back to the living room. I sat down in one of the chairs and he sat in the other. We drank.

I said, "This is decidedly tastier than the Seaside's."

"I'm known for my martinis. Someone once named them silver bullets."

I wondered who the someone was. I hadn't heard of his going out with any of the other single women teachers at Millbridge. Was his sex life supplied by Hull girls? I said, "Not known in quite the same way as your mother and her pies."

"Not quite."

I looked at the wall of books and thought of the fifteen cartons of my books which I'd stored in Lucy's attic, unable to make myself sell them.

He got up and went to the fireplace and pushed newspaper under the logs in it. "I guess it's cold enough now for a fire," he said, lighting it. He stopped by my chair and offered me a cigarette and lit that, too.

We drank and watched the fire. I tried to think myself backward, to make myself new again, and I remembered going mountain climbing with Ned and Lucy when Susan was so young Ned toted her in his pack basket, and I remembered going blueberrying and how Susan and I would get bitten by black flies; black fly bites, I remembered, and the oddly luscious moment of discovering that dry crust of blood behind my ear. Then I heard Lucy saying, "The only way to carry a bowl of soup without spilling, Emily, is not to look at it," and then I remembered playing dress-up in Lucy's clothes. I remembered a red-and-green-flowered silky dress with pads sewn in its shoulders, the dress hitched up by a cracked patent-leather belt, I remembered clumpy high-heeled shoes and an enormous old pocketbook which smelled of lipstick and tobacco crumbs.

And then I remembered a perfect moment: a winter day; I was warm in the big chair in the living room, and I had a new Nancy Drew book and a deviled ham sandwich (with mayonnaise, on squishy white bread).

But here I was in Cliff's living room. The red flames rushed upward, the wood snapped, and Cliff deliberately stood up, came over, and sat down on the arm of my chair and took the drink from my hand, put it on the little table, stubbed out my cigarette in the ashtray, and began to kiss me.

And we were on the glowing rug, and I started to unzip my dress but he unzipped it and slipped it off.

"You don't wear a bra," he said. "I didn't think you did."

"No, not anymore," I said, and although my voice was breathless, for a moment my mind veered away again, as always, to David. At Brompton when I used to wear a padded bra, he was fond of draping it across his head like earphones and whistling like John Wayne in *The High and the Mighty*.

Cliff said, "You're lovely."

I had thought he would look funny, without his clothes on, with his face still clothed in his beard. He didn't look funny at all.

"You're lovely," he kept saying. "You're lovely." He was very slow and easy, as David was, and he kissed my breasts until I thought I'd go crazy, and then his head was between my legs and I caught his thick curls in my fingers and I came and came and came, and then he was surging into me and the slowness was gone, he was pounding against me, and again I came, and shudderingly he came.

We lay together until the hot film of sweat began to evaporate and, despite the fire, to chill. I kissed his shoulder. "Where's your bathroom?"

"Off the kitchen." He kissed me. "You're lovely."

Stickily he retreated out of me.

I said, "I do think there ought to be a more dignified way of going about this," and clamped my hands between my legs and ran for the bathroom. I sat on the toilet and mopped up. The bathroom was very small and narrow, with a ceiling as high as the other rooms, and the bathtub was so small I imagined that in it he must look like a Western movie hero in a washtub, beard all a-lather. I used his washcloth to wash myself, and his towel to dry. Then I ran back to the living room for my clothes.

He was still lying on the rug, the fire flickering.

"Hi," he said.

"Hi."

He watched while I put on my underpants and dress and sandals.

He said, "Can you stay the night?"

"First I'm going to cook us that supper," I said. I knelt down and touched his beard. "Yes. I'll stay."

THE HEAD OF THE DEPARTMENT

AND THEN it was May, warm May, and there were apple blossoms and lilacs and daffodils and dandelions and violets, and the world was fluffy with boughs of leaves, and robins bounced across green lawns.

I spent more time with Cliff than at my apartment. After school we would drive old roads in the cream puff Volvo to see springtime, and at his apartment we'd have martinis and I'd cook supper and we would correct papers and talk about my lesson plans and watch reruns on television. Sometimes I eventually went home, but I stayed the night often enough to buy a separate supply of necessities: in his bathroom now were my hairbrush and comb, my face cream and body lotion and powder and lipstick and eye makeup and toothbrush and deodorant and razor, and even my Tampax.

Cliff solemnly opened the box of Tampax and took out the directions. He read aloud, "If you're a new user of Tampax, let me help you!"

I said, "I always wonder where they think we'll put it if they don't tell us. In our ear?"

On the Tuesday nights when I had my class he took me to Durham and waited the two hours in the library, reading. On Friday nights we went to the drive-in theater which showed skin flicks. On Saturdays I did both our laundries in the brand-new laundry room in the apartment building, and he took first my car and then his to the automatic car wash. I gave him a banjo concert. We had suppers of the fried shrimp appetizer, and virtuously nothing more, at the Chinese restaurant. On Sundays we went for Sunday drives and had Sunday dinners of ice cream cones at the UNH Dairy Bar. We never went to the ocean.

But the first Saturday in May I had been with Kaykay and Grace. In Grace's car, because it was the most comfortable, we drove to the Jordan Marsh in Maine. The Bridal Salon was very intimidating, with long mirrors and fragile furniture, and the elegant clerk was intimidating also, except not to Kaykay, who, her usual brisk self, scrutinized the sample dresses, interrogated the clerk—"Chantilly lace," they said to each other, "bishop sleeves, lantern sleeves, bell skirt, chapel train"—and chose a lacy gown that seemed to me so unreal it might be something I'd dreamed of in my childhood, a storybook gown.

All the samples were size ten. Round and round the room, a parade of white and pastel gowns, brides and bridesmaids, all the same size.

With Grace, the authority, as consultant, we chose bridesmaids' gowns of soft yellow—"lemon organza," said Grace and Kaykay and the clerk. In the dressing room, I thought that at least this dress seemed more familiar, somewhat like the "formals" I'd worn, escorted by David, to high school proms and to fraternity dances at Brompton, although most of those had been strapless dresses with net stoles which puffed out around your shoulders. David in a dinner jacket. I could almost smell gardenias.

I didn't fit the gown; I am size seven.

Grace and I ordered ours, and Kaykay ordered one for her sister who would be matron of honor, and then, while Kaykay and the clerk were discussing veils, I looked over and saw Grace staring at the wedding gown Kaykay had chosen. Grace's hands were clenched, a muscle jumped in her jawbone, and her face was as white as the lace.

When we got home, I drove to Cliff's, and we sat in the wicker chairs on his porch and drank our martinis. The smell of lilac bushes was hot and purple and achingly sweet.

I had to be with him, I couldn't be alone. For now that I knew where David was, if I were alone I would drive to Pleasantfield to see the school where David taught and the place where David lived, and maybe, maybe see David.

• • •

This Friday night, however, we didn't go to a skin flick. We had supper, and then I came back to the apartment to help Grace, while Kaykay was at Bob's, write out the invitations for the bridal shower we were giving Kaykay. We finished by nine thirty. I made ham and Swiss cheese sandwiches for the picnic Cliff and I would have tomorrow when we went fishing in North Riverton, and Grace and I discussed the food and drink to serve at the shower. Grace was very knowledgeable about showers, so, although I preferred the idea of straight booze and canapés, I eventually agreed with her on fruit punches, hard and soft, and little sandwiches and cakes.

Then we each had a scotch and watched some of *Bracken's World*, and then Grace took a sleeping pill and went to bed. I bathed, put on a nightgown, made another drink, turned out all the lights, except the lamp on the bedside table, and got in bed to begin rereading *The Old Man and the Sea*. My turn had come to have the copies of the book for one of my freshmen classes, and I must start teaching it next week. I opened it.

There was a loud splintering bang in the living room. I spilled my drink on the bedclothes, and when I looked up a man was standing in my doorway.

He said, "I'm going to fuck you. I'm going to give you a fucking like you never had."

This wasn't happening.

He said, "I'm going to fuck you like you've never been fucked."

I was freezing, I was sweating. An ice cube melted against my leg. Very carefully I put the book on the bedside table and got out of bed.

I said, "Would you like a drink first?" My voice was shaky, but it was a voice. "You made me spill my drink."

He kept looking at me, and I realized how short and how transparent the nightgown was. The Levi's I'd been wearing were lying on Kaykay's bed. I reached slowly for them and slowly began to put them on.

He said, "I'm going to fuck you."

Grace, I thought, should I yell at Grace, tell her to lock her door, to go out her window for help? She wouldn't hear me, she'd taken that sleeping pill. What about the other people in the other apartments, would they hear? I tried to see the man's face, but the hall was dark.

I tucked in my nightgown and zipped the fly of the Levi's. I said, "Why don't I get us a drink?" Hopeless, hopeless, helpless, helpless, why in God's name didn't I take a karate course instead of Analysis of Teaching? Teaching. I assumed a stronger teacher's voice than I ever used and said firmly, "We're both going to have a drink, and I do hope you've got some cigarettes because I would like one," and walked toward the door in much the same way I used to walk into elementary school battles when I was a kid, holding myself rigid, my eyes open but blind.

He stepped aside and I walked into the living room.

He said, "Don't turn on the lights."

I headed for the kitchen. There were knives in the kitchen. No. He'd get the knife away from me and kill me as well as fuck me. I said, "How on earth can I make the drinks without a light? Don't be ridiculous," and the telephone rang.

I was close enough to it to pick it up immediately, before he could tell me not to.

"Hello, Emily, this is Cliff. You're up, I was afraid I'd wake you, but I couldn't keep from calling. I miss you."

"Yes," I said.

The man stood uncertain, watching me. I was beginning to be able to see that he was younger than I'd thought, maybe twenty-five or so. His jacket and trousers were dark; he wore desert boots. Who was he?

Cliff was saying, "There'll be mayflowers at the brook, I'll show you where the mayflowers are."

"Yes," I said.

There was a pause. Then he said, "Emily, is something wrong?"

"Yes."

"What is it?"

"Yes."

"Do you want me to come over? Right now?"

"Yes."

"Jesus God," he said and hung up. I listened to the dial tone.

The man said, "Come on, we're leaving." He seized my arm.

"All right," I said, twisting loose, talking very fast, "I'll come with you, but I'm not going anywhere with all this goopy cream on my face, what would people think? I'll just go clean it off and put on a shirt," and I walked into the hall, opened Grace's bedroom door, stepped in, and locked it behind me.

"Grace. Grace, wake up. *Please*."

She didn't. I shook her hard and still she didn't, and I looked at the door and thought frantically, if he can break the living room door he can break this. Should I stay here with Grace or should I get out, is he after me in particular or any girl? Grace slept with the window closed, and the room was warm and smelled serenely of face cream and sleep. What should I do, what should I do? I slammed open the window. Thank God, the windows were new; I never could work old ones. I sat on the windowsill, swung my legs over, and jumped down.

The nighttime landscape of rubble, the silent empty trucks looming like monsters.

I ran across the newly seeded lawn and hid behind a pile of cinder blocks. From the swamp behind me thousands of spring peepers shrilled in pulse beats as fast as mine.

The people in the other apartments must have gone to bed, for their windows were dark, all except one which showed between curtains the blue light of a television screen. A car started up somewhere and drove off. I peeked out, but it was too far away for me to see more than its headlights merging into the other headlights on the road that became the Miracle Mile.

Then another set of headlights drove in, very fast, and I saw the familiar Volvo shape. I ran toward it, the car stopped, Cliff leaped out and grabbed me.

"Emily, what's going on?"

"Some guy broke in, I think he's gone now, a car drove off."

"Are you okay?"

"Yes."

"You wait here."

So I waited while he went into the building, and I tried to slow my breathing.

"All right," he called. "He's gone."

The living room door was ripped open.

Cliff said, examining it, "These goddamned flimsy new buildings. Emily, your feet are bare, you'll catch your death."

"Better than a fate worse than," I said, and started laughing and shaking. Cliff put his arm around me and held me against him as we walked into the kitchen. He began making drinks.

"Is Grace okay?" he asked.

"Oh, God, she's locked in, I locked her door and went out her window," I said, and started laughing again. "I'd better come back in her window."

"I'll do it."

"Well, she slept through all this, so I guess she'll sleep through that."

"Did you know the guy? What did he look like?"

"It was dark, but I don't think I've ever seen him before. Noticed him, anyway."

"Did he say anything?"

"He said he was going to fuck me. He was rather tiresomely repetitious about it." I took the glass he gave me; the ice rattled loudly when I tried to drink. "Was he after me, and if he was, how'd he know I live here? Has he been watching me in some store or something, did he follow me?"

"He wasn't a student?"

"No, he was older."

"I think you should call the police."

I opened a cupboard and swiped a pack of Salems from Kaykay's carton. We lit cigarettes; he looked up the number of the police station for me and dialed and handed me the receiver. While I reported, he went out the door and came back through Grace's room. The cop sounded bored.

When I hung up I said, "He asked if I wanted someone sent over, I told him I guessed not. I think he thought I was lying about the whole thing." And I was suddenly more angry at that than I was afraid of the man who'd broken in, and the anger steadied me.

"Jesus God," Cliff said. "What if I hadn't phoned?"

I said, "I'd've probably tried to kick him in the balls and got beat up instead," but with the steadiness came a curious sense of triumph. I had been handling the situation somewhat, and perhaps I might have gone on handling it.

Most likely not. And when Cliff said, "I'd better spend the night here," the fear returned at the thought of the man's return, and I looked at Cliff, tall and solid and bearded, and said, "Yes."

He said, "Before we leave tomorrow, you ought to call the building manager and ask about getting the lock and door repaired."

"I intend to," I said. Then I said, "Thank you for coming over."

"Oh, Christ," he said.

We finished our drinks. I said, "Would you like to use my toothbrush?"

The spilled drink had dried. We undressed. Cliff wasn't wearing any underwear, he had just pulled on pants and a sweater after talking to me, and he'd already emptied his pockets at his apartment, so on my bureau there was no jumble of their contents, as there was at his place, as there had been on David's bureau always: cigarettes, wallet, keys, handkerchief, coins. Here were only the car keys. I missed seeing the rest.

Cliff didn't get into Kaykay's bed. He got into bed with me and held me close. We didn't say anything for a long time. I listened to my heart still racing, and I couldn't go to sleep.

Cliff said, "Look. Let's get married."

"*What?*"

He laughed, but when he spoke his voice, though joking, was embarrassed. "It's not such an outrageous idea as all that, is it?"

Yes, yes, it was.

He said, "We'd live in North Riverton and you could write."

"I'm through writing."

"Well," he said. "You could teach. I've been trying for weeks to figure out a way to say this, and I haven't been able to, but there's another English opening in North Riverton. You'd have better classes than here, we could divvy up the college prep classes and you could have some seniors and juniors for a change. And we'd be working together."

I got out of bed, turned on the lamp, and fetched the cigarettes from the kitchen. Cliff sat up in bed. I lit a cigarette and handed him the pack and climbed back in beside him. I balanced the ashtray on my knees.

I said, "Is it because of tonight? You don't have to protect me, it'll probably never happen again."

"Emily."

"Say I applied for the job and got it. Why couldn't everything keep on like here?"

"North Riverton isn't Millbridge or Hull. The townsfolk haven't been made so tolerant as people down here, there're no UNH kids, graduate students, whatever, shacking up all over the place. If they found out we were living together, or damn near living together, we'd get fired."

"Oh." The same thing no doubt would happen in Thornhill.

He said, "Anyway, I want to marry you."

Stunned, flattered, scared, bewildered.

He said, "We could wait until school is over, if you'd rather. We could get engaged."

"We're too old to get engaged."

"Wouldn't you like a ring?"

I thought of the symbols David had given me in high school and college, first his little gold football on a chain around my neck, then his fraternity pin on my breast. I said, "My hands are hideous."

He said, "I'll give you a hideous ring, to match."

"I'm a lousy teacher."

"Not so lousy as you think you are."

"I'm not?"

"No. The only thing is, the pay is lower than here. You must be making six thousand now, and next year with the new pay scale you'll make about sixty-five hundred, right? Well, maybe I could wring sixty-two for you out of Matthew, but I'm afraid that's about all."

It seemed plenty. I still judged salaries by the forty-one hundred dollars which had been David's starting salary in Thornhill.

Cliff said, "When I was at my interview, I picked up an application form for you, just in case."

I didn't say anything. I couldn't think what to say.

He said, "I want to live with you in North Riverton. I want to work there with you."

"I might not get the job."

"You'll get it."

I said, "I can't think straight."

David. David.

Cliff said, "There's nothing to think about. We'll get married and go to North Riverton and live happily ever after until we're buried under A-frames."

A direct question: "How come you never got married before?"

"Just lucky, I guess."

"No, how come?"

"Well, North Riverton High School wasn't exactly teeming with the women of my dreams, so I never got involved that far with any girl, and then at the university there was a girl, but after a couple of years I all of a sudden realized I didn't like her, and then there was the army, and then after teaching for a few years, I don't know, I got into the habit of being on my own, and when I saw what other people were putting up with, mortgages and washing machines and kids' dentist bills and God knows what, I began to count my blessings."

"So why me?"

"How the hell should I know? It must be your hideous hands and your dirty feet."

"Oh, Jesus, they're filthy, aren't they, I completely forgot—"

"Emily, Emily," he said, laughing, and started to kiss me.

"Our cigarettes!" I said. We put them out and looked at each other. I said, "Remember that time at the housewarming party, you were drunk and made that pass at me right on this bed?"

"Don't I. I didn't dare ask you out for three months afterward. And I had to try to be a good guy and big pal and not leer at you in the teachers' room."

And now we were beginning to have our own history together.

But would he ask about David? He had never mentioned David, not even that day at the beach.

"Emily," he said. "I love you."

This was something else he'd never said. I stroked the smooth skin of his shoulder and the curly hair on his chest. I realized that sleep was dragging at my eyelids. God, I was tired. "Let me think it over," I said. I put my head on his shoulder, and he placed the ashtray on the table and turned off the lamp. It was snug and safe here with him. To thank him, I said, "I love you."

• • •

There were little silver umbrellas on white paper, there were silver ribbons, there were voices twittering over all the presents as Kaykay, sitting on the rug, unwrapped each one, admired it, and handed it along to be admired by everyone else. Jam and mustard pots, sheets and towels, salt and pepper shakers, salad bowls, they circulated the room and returned to Kaykay until she was surrounded by them, highball glasses, mixing bowls, chip-and-dip bowls, and casserole dishes. Grace gave her an electric carving knife. I gave her *The Graham Kerr Cookbook*, because it wasn't on her lists.

While I ladled out the hard punch, and Grace ladled the soft, I remembered David's and my going down to Lexington with Susan and John and Pam and Lucy to sort things out when Ma died. The old streets, the trees, the big white house with a vine-darkened porch. Indoors, the smell was the familiar smell of overstuffed chairs and china closets. On the hall table was the glove box which had been my great-great-grandfather's, and beside it, as always, was the mail. A letter I had written a few days before lay on top, unopened.

At first Lucy had broken down; no longer efficient, she wandered lost and weepy around the house. So the rest of us had had to begin making the decisions. All the things, all the things, everything Ma and Pop had treasured for sixty years together, from their wedding presents all the way to the TV tables David and I had given them their last Christmas. Sixty years of accumulation.

I remembered how Susan and I walked through the house, Pam trotting along behind us. First hesitantly, then more courageously, we put tags on the things for Lucy and the things for ourselves. The good pieces of furniture, the books, the cut glass, the china and silverware and linen and doilies, the new vacuum cleaner Ma had just bought, the sewing machine and pictures. And we chose the things we loved, the candy dish still full of hard candies, as it always was, a fringed lamp, snapshot albums, a gold thimble, and the scrapbook of sample scraps from Ma's wedding gown and trousseau and her brides-maids' dresses.

After the divorce, I gave Susan all of my things of Ma's. And now they would someday be Pam's, and then Pam's children's.

Grace was saying to Joanne Webster, the art teacher, "As you can see, we're going to be having a vacancy here. You wouldn't by any chance be looking for a new apartment?"

"Well, yes," Joanne said, selecting a pink petit four, "but the trouble is, I'm looking in Massachusetts, I'm going down to Massachusetts, I've had it here."

"Oh," Grace said.

There wasn't any funeral; Ma hadn't wanted one, after the ordeal of Pop's. She was cremated, like Pop.

I said to Grace, "There'll be the new teachers, they'll be frantic for apartments."

"I suppose."

And the debate continued within me: How could I bear another year in this apartment with Grace and some girl who would replace Kaykay, another year and another year and another—

I had been extremely startled when our marriage had brought presents to Brompton. I hadn't even thought about presents, just about living with David at last, but the presents came, from relatives, from friends of Lucy's and friends of Ma and Pop's. In our shabby apartment David and I would unwrap them wonderingly, a silver cake plate, towels, a bean pot, candlesticks. A silver bon-bon dish, too; we'd unwrapped it, laughed and laughed, eaten our supper of tuna wiggle, and David had picked up his books and gone off to work at the gas station while I washed the dishes and settled back down at the kitchen table, which was also our desk, to do our Advanced Grammar homework.

Bob came in as the women began to leave. "Were you surprised?" he asked Kaykay.

"Oh, yes!" she said, although I didn't think she really had been. "Come see everything. Good-bye, Barbara, and thank you again, good-bye, Darlene, thank you, good-bye, Cynthia, good-bye, Joanne, good-bye good-bye thank you thank you thank you."

When they all had left, Kaykay and Bob knelt on the rug and she showed him each present. Grace and I picked up the paper plates and crumpled napkins and began to clear off the counter. Grace ate one of the leftover sandwiches and stood watching them.

I looked around the avocado kitchen, seeing instead our funny kitchen in Brompton, where the sink was tacked with an oilcloth skirt and the refrigerator wore its motor on top.

I made a drink and wished that Cliff would hurry up and arrive as he'd promised. All at once I wanted desperately to get out of here.

"Let's leave the dishes," I said to Grace. "I'll do them tomorrow."

There was a knock on the door, and Cliff came in. "How'd it go?"

I said, "Fine, lots of loot." We kissed.

"Come see!" Kaykay said, and he went over and admired everything. He took a swallow of my drink and asked, "Where would you like to go?"

"I don't know," I said, and then I did. Someplace not white and silver; someplace dark and dingy. "Let's go to Dot's, I haven't been there for months."

"Lord, I haven't been there in a year. All right, Dot's it is."

We finished my drink. As I put on my jacket, Kaykay looked up from studying a casserole dish and said, astonishingly, "Kind of depressing, isn't it?"

Bob said, "Well, thanks a heap."

"Oh, you know what I mean," she said. "Can we come along with you two?"

"Sure," we said. I said to Grace, "Come with us."

After a moment, Grace said, "Thanks, but I'll stay here."

Kaykay said, "Do you mind the mess, Grace? I'll pack it tomorrow morning."

"No, I don't mind," Grace said.

We followed Bob's car. The cool June evening. Downtown was still busy with the last of the Friday-night shoppers, the neon signs brilliant in the twilight.

Even though classes were over at UNH, Dot's was jumping, the jukebox bellowing, the pinball machine crashing, actors roaring accusations at each other from the television, and people yelling and laughing.

"Hi, kiddies!" Dot shouted. "Jesus Christ, Emily and Kaykay, I was beginning to think you'd left town. Hi there, Bob, hi"—she paused only briefly before she came up with his name—"hi there, Cliff. Buds for everyone?"

She tramped out to the kitchen, and we sat at the bar. "My God," Cliff said. "She remembered my name."

I said, "She's a computer bank of names, I've seen her greet old alumni like they were just in here the day before," and over the noise there was the high shrill bark of a puppy. Tiny and black, it emerged from under a booth and bobbed and barked at the occupants, demanding attention.

Dot plunked down our Budweisers. "Anybody want a glass?"

"No, that's fine," we said.

I said, "Whose puppy is that?"

"You want one?" she asked. "Larry over there, the kid with the mustache and the striped pants, the fellow he works for was going to drown them—"

"Oh, no!" Kaykay cried.

I said, "Them?" and then saw another puppy, blond, sound asleep in the corner.

"So Larry took them," Dot said, "and now he's trying to give them away. Want one?"

Cliff glanced at me. A puppy; he was offering me a puppy, too, as well as North Riverton.

I said, "My sister has a border collie. Do you like border collies?" and I remembered how once I had seen a flock of grackles land in the field across the road from Susan's house and Bruce jump up from the doorstep, check the road, and dash across to chase them. The grackles flew away, yet Bruce kept running. The sun was shining on the green field, and Bruce was running, no reason for his running now except pleasure, a gay rhythmic lope, beautiful, which sang that he did not know there was anything else but life.

Cliff said, "Yes, I like border collies, we had a couple when I was a kid."

Bob said, "Hey, Dot, how about a bag of Beer Nuts?"

She yanked one off the display card. "The wedding must be almost any day now, huh?"

"The twentieth," Kaykay said. "The day after school's over."

Dot said, "Well, if I don't see you before, I wish you all the happiness in the world." She said this formally. Then she looked at Cliff and me speculatively.

"Another Pabst, Dot!" somebody yelled.

The closer the time came, the more I didn't want to go to Brompton for Kaykay's wedding, not even with Cliff as a buffer against our years there.

The black puppy pranced over to investigate us, and Kaykay picked him up. She and Bob began talking about Witherell; they had taken jobs there and found an apartment. She was saying, "And if we like the jobs, we've got to buy a house. I hate to rent, it's such an awful waste of money, and unless it's a new apartment, there's the mess people leave and you find their bobby pins in the dust."

Cliff's hands, the hands like David's, toyed with his beer bottle, making thumbprints on its coldness. "My mother phoned tonight," he said. "She and my father have pretty much come to a decision. They're going to move into town. She says she's fed up with being stuck out in the country, she wants a smaller house she can take care of more easily and have a new stove and all that and visit her friends in town and everything, but I think the real reason is that the place has got too much for my father."

"Oh, Cliff, I'm sorry."

"She wanted to know if I wanted to live there. If not, they'll rent it." He gave me a cigarette. "We could live there, Emily."

I said, "I have a thing about cigarettes, I like to light my own."

"Why didn't you say so?"

The match he tossed at the grimy ashtray ignited a strand of red cellophane. I poured beer on it. "I don't know," I said. I felt very brave, and continued, "I don't like chairs pulled out for me, either, and I hate to wait while you open a door for me, it makes me feel like a well-trained dog. Which that one isn't," I said. The blond puppy had awakened and was creating a small puddle.

"You little bastard!" Dot bellowed, and rushed out from behind the bar waving paper towels. "Larry, this damn puppy of yours—"

Kaykay said, "Dot, you're scaring him," and handed Bob the black puppy and slid down off the barstool and scooped up the blond puppy just as Dot started shoving his nose in the puddle. "It's all right," Kaykay crooned, "she's a meanie, you'll learn, won't you, sweetie?"

Cliff said, "All you had to do was say so," and watched me light my cigarette. My diversion was ended. He said, "What about the house?"

The house I'd sought in Thornhill. And Susan had said that of course I must take back my things of Ma's whenever I wanted, she would just look after them, I could get them and probably his mother would leave some things of hers or his grandparents' and they would merge, and we would have a home and a tradition. No more mock-traditional furniture in a brick-faced building surrounded by other brick-faced buildings overlooking the Miracle Mile.

And North Riverton was in the part of New Hampshire I liked best, and he was the teacher I liked best to work with, so why wasn't I saying okay?

He said, "As my mother pointed out, the place'll be mine someday, anyway."

"Do they really want to move?"

"Yes. I believe they really do." He made another thumbprint. "We'd keep it just the way it is, we'd never sell any of it."

Kaykay was back on the barstool. Stroking her puppy, she leaned around Bob who was stroking the black puppy, and said,

"Emily, what do you think, how long should I work before we have a baby?"

"Good Lord, I don't know."

"I think a year," she said. "Bob thinks two years."

Bob said, "And that means it'll be a year."

I hadn't mentioned Cliff's proposal to Kaykay or Grace, but Kaykay had seen me studying the application form and asked me what school it was for, and now she said suddenly, "You two, what you ought to do is get married and have a baby and stop all this nonsense, like us."

Bob said, "For God's sake, Kathleen Harrison, mind your own business."

"A baby?" I said. I looked at Cliff, stupefied.

He said, "Maybe I'm too elderly." He was, I'd learned, thirty-four, a year older than David.

Bob guffawed. "Hey, Dot, how about another round and some more Beer Nuts, and haven't you got some milk or something for the puppies?"

While he and Cliff argued over who was paying this round and Kaykay set a bowl of milk on the floor, I tried to sort my thoughts out of a strange tranquillity spreading over me. A baby. I had never ever wanted a baby. Back then, it would have been a nuisance, like unwanted company, when all I wanted was David, and it would have interfered with writing. Now? Why not now? I could stay home and be married and have a baby to take care of. I thought of Ann carrying David's.

Cliff looked up at the television and hummed, "Now the day is over, night is drawing nigh." Then he said, "I gather if you didn't have any, you don't want any."

"Do you?"

"It'd be okay with me."

We wouldn't sell any of the farm, and someday it would be the baby's, even if it had to be only a summer place.

What would Cliff and I look like, all mixed up together?

"When?" I said.

"Whenever you want. Never, if you don't want." He laughed and said, "What a peculiar place to be having this discussion," and we listened to the pandemonium around us.

For the first time in my life I tried to picture myself pregnant. A taut balloon. Inside me, something from a physiology book, a polliwog growing eyes and arms and toenails. Once Pam asked Susan, "When I was in your tummy, did I get food on my face when you ate?" I thought of the new clothes I could buy, those mysterious skirts with elastic pouches. I thought of baby things to buy, and remembered saving up enough money to buy Susan, for Pam, an electric food warmer decorated with a picture of Little Miss Muffet and an amiable spider.

David and I had driven over to the Cate hospital to see Susan and the pink bundle named Pamela. On the bedside table, among the gifts of flowers and frilly little dresses and bonnets, was a copy of *Good-bye to All That*, Robert Graves's book about World War I. I'd said, "What on earth is this doing here?" and Susan laughed. "The trenches," she said. "To put things in perspective. John read it to me while I was in labor."

And I remembered a couple of years later, Susan and I were shopping in Cate's colonial-façaded supermarket, and she said, "I never thought I'd be lugging around crayons and dog biscuits in my pocketbook." She smiled her sweet smile, but her tone was bleak. The shopping cart contained Pam, short legs dangling, as well as groceries. Abruptly, Susan halted the cart beside a table of geraniums for sale. Red geraniums. She looked at them for a long time. "When I was in the fifth grade," she said at last, "my school desk was near the windows and every day I sat and watched a geranium dying beside me. Finally I couldn't stand it and sneaked it home in my lunch box. Remember? Lucy gave me holy hell and made me apologize to Miss Wheeler, but Miss Wheeler said that if I could revive it, I could keep it. It revived. I was mighty proud." And what revived at that moment was her interest in plants, for she bought two geraniums, and from then on it was her passion, she studied plants, she saved every spare cent to buy plants, and she manufactured a new Susan who was not merely Pam's mother, Bruce's mistress, John's wife. Susan was plants.

Now Kaykay, having watched the puppies lap milk, let them scamper off and hoisted herself up on the stool. "Does everyone get panicky and depressed and all that, just before they get married? Did you?" she asked me. She reached for her beer. I'd never until now seen Kaykay blush. She said hastily, "I mean, it's stupid, here I've known this idiot two years, I certainly know what I'm getting into—"

"So do I," Bob said, grinning, and Kaykay said, "Oh, go to hell, it's just all of a sudden I don't know—I want, I want—I don't know. Those damn casserole dishes. Thank you again for the Galloping Gourmet's cookbook, Emily; if it had been *A Hundred and One Ways to Cook Hamburg*, I'd've burst into tears." She brightened. "Look at him." The black puppy had come back and was licking her toes in her sandals.

She picked him up. "I'll be all right once the wedding's over with, I'll be all right."

When we left, the black puppy left with Kaykay and Bob. They drove off to Bob's apartment.

What am I going to do? I thought, as we drove along Main Street, the stores dark and silent now. Everything was dark. We drove up the one-way street between the factories, and nothing was alive but the lunch wagon, a rattletrap van parked in an alley, where people from the bars down the side streets waited in line for sobering-up food. FRENCH FRIES 19¢ STEAMED HOT DOGS 25¢. Cliff swore, and stepped on the brake. Out in front of us lurched a thin man followed by a fat woman wearing a ragged cardigan over a cotton dress. The man was shoving a hot dog into his mouth, and in his other hand he gripped a greasy paper bag, and the woman was screaming at him. "You asshole!" she screamed. "Can't you wait till we get home?" He opened the bag and took out another hot dog and crammed that into his mouth, and she kept screaming, "You fucking asshole!" as they staggered down the dark street past the old brick factories.

• • •

Champagne, at last. So very much champagne. Kaykay had said, "The biggest sum of money spent for my sister's wedding was spent on oceans of champagne, that's what made it such a huge success, and that's the way mine's going to be." It was, although to me, terrified of making a mistake, the ceremony itself was a hushed white-and-yellow trance, and even immediately afterward I couldn't remember anything about it except the one real thing that happened, the little flower girl's keeling over in a faint, and the instant reaction of her mother, Kaykay's sister, the matron of honor. She dropped her bouquet and picked up the child and handed her to her husband, who came running from a pew and took her outside, all so swiftly and quietly that Kaykay in front of us, eyes on the minister, didn't know what happened until we told her later. Which proved that Kaykay too was in a trance; would the ceremony be to her as dim a memory as a performance in a senior play in high school?

But at the reception in the Twombly Park Clubhouse, there were the oceans of champagne, and people drank and danced and drank and drank and drank, and the flower girl contentedly munched wedding cake. Grace, very flushed, danced with ushers and with Kaykay's father. And I danced with Cliff, great exaggerated swooping glides around the room, and we laughed and laughed at each other. The afternoon was hot, and the smell of heated deodorant mingled with the smell of flowers and perfume.

At the house, Kaykay threw her bouquet toward Grace, but one of the other girls in the shrieking throng caught it. And then Kaykay kissed the black puppy good-bye and gave him to her mother to take care of until her return, and Kaykay and Bob drove off toward Nova Scotia in a storm of rice, an inappropriate sign on their bumper announcing JUST MARRIED, AMATEUR NIGHT.

Cliff put our suitcases and my garment bag bloated with lemon organza in the Volvo and said, "What we ought to do is go take a swim somewhere and cool off before we drive home. And douse the champagne. You brought a bathing suit, didn't you?"

"Yes," I said. Kaykay had suggested it, thinking a swim after the wedding rehearsal last night might be nice, but instead we all went drinking at the Brompton Tavern Cocktail Lounge. David and I had gone there once in a while when we were hungry for television; we would sit at the bar and try to nurse our single beers through at least one show. Last night I had sat in a festive booth and drunk gin and tonics.

"Where's the beach?" Cliff asked.

"I don't know, somewhere at Lake Samoset. We always swam at the college camp on Hunkins Lake."

We got into the car and looked at each other, hot and dizzy. He said, "How about there, then?"

A test. "All right," I said.

He waited. "Where is it?"

"Oh," I said. "Drive back past the campus."

The campus at the far end of Main Street had grown crowded with new buildings, confusing memory. Somewhere in there was the auditorium with the old buff-colored mural showing settlers being attacked by Indians, and over the proscenium two admonitions that David always used to delight in, especially because they contradicted each other: ENTER TO LEARN, GO FORTH TO SERVE and IF YOU DO THIS, YOU CAN'T DO THAT. Gone was the yellow frame cottage where the English Department held its classes. We'd sit on the porch steps to smoke a last cigarette before a class began, and in the winter the snowbanks around the steps looked like ashtrays of butts. What had been a new building in our time, the Campus Club, a cinder-block cube containing a lunch counter, shiny Formica tables, racks of paperbacks, and Brompton sweatshirts and beer mugs, now seemed seedy. We had complained then that it resembled a supermarket, and we had loudly mourned the old Campus Club, made from an abandoned classroom, a dirty yet intimate place.

I said, "That's the president's house. Turn right."

And as we drove out of town, past gas stations and trailers, I remembered my Brompton sweatshirt which in Thornhill had become my housework sweatshirt. With the years, its navy blue washed away to a pale lavender stained with copper polish and Clorox, and its softness grew thin and stiff. Eventually the lettering almost disappeared, and a few red flakes were all that was left of BROMPTON STATE COLLEGE and the school emblem; when the words were bright and new, I had worn the sweatshirt inside out. Most everybody did.

After a hamburger stand, we turned and drove to the dirt road that encircled the small lake, the camps like children playing ring-around-the-rosy. And there it was, a dilapidated shack built high for the view.

Our graduation party had been held here. At first David and I had thought we wouldn't bother to go, sensing it wouldn't be a good party but an anticlimax. Recovering from finals, still unable to believe that our sixteen years of school were over, we sat dazed on the steps of our apartment house and brushed flies from our beer cans and idly discussed whether or not we should, after all, go. Finally we decided to, because it was the last party.

When we got there, the party had begun; people were swimming in the lake, and clouds of smoke rose from the stone fireplace on the lawn. We went down to the little beach, and David ran splashing in while I waded out slowly. The sun was setting, making a yellow road across the lake.

I dived, and as always was surprised that I couldn't stay under as long as I could when I was younger, and I came up swallowing water. "Goddamned cigarettes," I said. I dived again, and this time when I came up too soon I turned over on my back and floated. There was a piece of moon in the sky.

David surfaced near me, choking, his eyelashes stiff and starry with water. "Cigarettes," he said. "I'll never live to be thirty."

"You look like Bambi."

We floated together, and I tried to understand that school at last had ended, but I couldn't, so I thought about the times at the lake in Saundersborough.

Raindrops began to plop around us.

"Oh, hell," David said.

Thunder boomed over the lake, and the rain poured down. We swam to shore and joined the stampede for the camp, and upstairs, in a bedroom where the window was broken and the mattresses on the bunks looked chewed by mice, we peeled off our bathing suits, dried ourselves, and put on our clothes. Then we went downstairs.

The porch was very long and crooked, high above the lake where somebody was still swimming. People sat in broken wicker chairs and put their feet up on the railing, and people sat on the railing, too, and someone was sleeping face down in the hammock. We went over to the picnic table that had been carried here from the lawn when the rain began, and out of the devastation of hard-boiled eggs and soggy hot dog rolls we unearthed the six-pack we'd brought. David opened a beer for me and wandered off. I found an empty chair and placed a damp cushion over the hole in its seat and sat down and watched the lightning.

Somebody said, "Kind of a washout, isn't it?"

The thunder seemed to be moving away, but the rain still streamed off the roof and splashed past the edge of the railing and thudded into the pine needles far below. I lit a cigarette and watched the fellow beside me squeeze a beer can until it buckled as he talked, and I decided I didn't like people who did that, although perhaps it was no worse than stripping wet labels off beer bottles, my habit. I sat and dozed and listened to the rain and the talk and the record player until I realized that my cushion had sunk into the hole in the chair, and frayed strands of cane surrounded me.

I grasped the railing and pulled myself out, and strolled over to the living room doorway. Lots of people were playing cards and dancing, one fellow steering in a small circle the girl who slept against his chest. The room smelled of cigarette smoke and wet canvas and beer. I couldn't see David. It occurred to me that he most likely was under the porch.

I went back to the picnic table for a couple more beers and a can opener. The porch stairs were wet and my hands were full; I felt I had accomplished a great feat when I reached the bottom safely. A few times before we were married and had a place of our own, David and I had lain here beneath the porch. I ducked under the stairs and found the broken slatting and crawled in. The pine needles and old leaves were dry.

"It's me," I said. "I brought some more beer, and I remembered the can opener."

The darkness moved. He said, "Good."

I sat beside him and looked through the crisscrossed slats at the sheen of the camp's lights on the black lake. After a time, the swimmer came out of the water, and bare feet slapped on the stairs. A car started up and drove off. Far over the lake I could see a rim of oily yellow lights from town, and now and then the airport beacon swept white across the sky.

David said, "I don't suppose I'll be able to change anything at Thornhill. For a while."

I lit a cigarette and scraped away pine needles until I could push the match head into the earth.

He said, "First-year teacher. I'll be expected to go along doing everything the way it's been done forever. I'll probably have to teach *Silas Marner* to the sophomores, and no doubt Mrs. Noyes will tell me to have my freshmen make soap carvings of *Evangeline*."

I said, "Thornhill's a lovely town."

"Oh, yes."

We had liked it more than any other town we'd seen during David's interviews.

I said, "And we were lucky to find a house. A house, not an apartment. An upstairs and a downstairs of our very own."

"Yes."

I thought about how we'd arrange our furniture in the house when we moved in next week, how the dining room would become my study when we could afford a desk, how I would have all the days for writing. All the days ahead, in our house in the north country.

David put his arm around my shoulder and took the cigarette from my fingers and smoked at it. "But after the first year," he said, "then maybe I can start doing things the way I want to. If I can get them to give me the money to buy a ton of novels, if I can try the writing-through-reading idea—"

He fell silent. We sat and listened to the rain on the lake.

• • •

Cliff dived and came up looking like Neptune.

"Well," he said. "That clears the head."

We treaded water. Children were screaming and splashing in front of the camps on either side of us.

I swam to shore while Cliff swam farther out, and I started to walk toward the porch, to see whether or not the slatting under the stairs was still broken, but then I turned back and sat down on the beach. I scooped up wet sand and let it dribble through my fingers, building up a castle foundation. This was the way to make the most delicate, most ethereal castles. You could make towers unbelievably fragile.

When Cliff swam in, I was working on the second tower.

I said, "It's a dribble castle."

He said, "I've been thinking. Instead of going back to Hull, why don't we drive up to Saundersborough? I'd like to meet Lucy."

I could feel the beads of water on my body disappearing into the heat of the sun.

"Well," I said. I hadn't been back to Saundersborough all year, and I hadn't seen Lucy since Pam's birthday party in Cate in March. "Okay."

We went up to the car, I tugged my beach towel out of my suitcase, and we took off our bathing suits and dried ourselves and got dressed, hidden by trees from the other camps.

As we drove north along the Connecticut River, Cliff said, "I wonder what they do to make wedding cake frosting so awful. This one tasted like margarine. It even looked like it, the old kind."

"The white kind?"

He glanced at me. "You mean you remember the old oleo?"

"Of course I do. It was white, and you had to beat the color in. Lucy had a wooden butter paddle she used. And then they came out with the kind in a plastic bag and it had a little orange dot you broke and you squished it in," I said, and stopped. This was what David and I reminisced about, the things we remembered from the time before we knew each other, and we would marvel at the similarities and differences. Now David would say, "My brother and I used to play catch with that oleo bag. We'd sit around listening to the radio and throwing the bag back and forth to work the color in."

What Cliff said was, "I've told my landlord I'm leaving by the end of this month, Emily."

I looked quickly out my open window for a distraction.

Cliff said, "From Saundersborough, we could drive on up to North Riverton and talk with my folks about moving into the house. We could spend the night."

There was a fence of twine around the garden beside a farm-house, and from the twine, like charms on a bracelet, dangled little aluminum pans which frozen meat pies are sold in. I said, "Is that a new kind of scarecrow?"

"Pepsi," he hummed, "Pepsi's got a lot to give," and then we drove on and on without talking.

We came into Saundersborough past the railroad yards. The late sun stretched down across the empty warehouses, the empty cindery tracks. Farther along was a bridge spanning the tracks, and when we were kids and heard a train coming, we would race here as fast as we could, feet pounding, hearts pounding, to wait poised on the bridge for the right moment, and just before the train passed beneath us we would suck up all the saliva in our mouths, lean far over the railing, and spit into the billowing smokestack. Spray would fly up, sooty smoke engulfed us, and as the train roared beneath us we would count the cars.

Later, there were diesel trains, and now there were hardly any trains at all.

Main Street was hot and gritty. Cliff stopped at a light, and I looked at the pastel display of summer colognes in the window of the drugstore. There used to be a soda fountain in that drugstore, and once Susan, at the age of eight, had got sick during a root beer float and had thrown up on the sidewalk outside. Right there, that very spot, and I had stood beside her, shocked and embarrassed, but when people came over to help, Susan and I began to run. Holding hands, Susan sobbing in humiliation, we ran all the way home to Lucy, who took Susan's temperature and gave her cambric tea. The soda fountain had been replaced a few years ago by a counter filled with Timex watches, transistor radios, and bedpans.

"Where to?"

"Oh." I kept forgetting he didn't know. "Straight ahead."

"Is that the elementary school?"

"Yes, where Lucy works, where I went to school." It was a gloomy dark-brick building; most of the time its windows were made incongruously cheerful with children's projects, paper pumpkins, turkeys, Christmas trees, valentines, Easter eggs, but now they were blankly black; school was over. I tried to see myself playing jump rope in the school yard, playing jacks on the school steps, and I tried to see David, whom I hadn't known then because he was older, playing marbles.

I said, "Have you been to the high school? Saundersborough didn't play North Riverton in anything, did we?"

"No, North Riverton's too small. We played Thornhill and such."

"Oh. Well, the high school's up that street, but we turn here. That's the ski factory. That's where Ned worked." At the time I didn't know how he had died, and I understood only that he had gone to work as usual after breakfast, just as Susan and I had gone to school, and that we had come home as usual but he never did. Yet I knew that whatever had happened was at the factory, and for years I didn't look at the factory when I walked past. I said, "It's grown a lot since then, of course."

Now the street was cooler, shaded by trees, welcome and familiar, but I remembered how menacing it could become in the winter when I was little, in the dark that always surprised me when I came out of the movie theater I had entered in daylight for a matinee. It was scary enough to walk home with Susan or Carol or somebody; alone, stark terror accompanied me, a certainty that there were things lurking behind the trees, watching me, waiting to jump out and grab me, and I was nearly hysterical with fear by the time I reached the light and warmth of home. I never told Lucy, however.

We drove past the street on which David's folks lived in the house I knew best after my home and Ma and Pop's. Another old house on a tree-shaded street, it had been cozy with friendly old furniture until, during the past ten years, his folks had started buying new colonial imitations, and the house had become so busy with gold eagles on magazine racks and canisters and wastebaskets, wrought-iron eagles over doors and on trivets, and calico eagles quilted into bedspreads, that David said to me he expected all the wings to begin beating at once someday and bear the house up toward the sun.

I smiled. He was very funny.

Cliff looked over at me. "Glad to be home?"

"Well."

The handsome old houses, the leisurely peaceful streets deep green under the old trees. More of the houses, it seemed, had been turned into apartment houses, curtains in their attic windows. I said, "Here we are," and we drove up the driveway to the big white colonial.

I said, "Lucy had it painted again, at last."

"It's quite a house."

We parked alongside the ell at the back. Lucy's Volkswagen was in the barn. I got out of the car and looked around the green yard. The garden had shrunk in the years since Susan and I left—Lucy had said, "I can't possibly eat all those vegetables by myself, and I can't give them away because everybody else has gardens, too"—and this summer there were only the raspberry bushes.

I opened the back door and we went into the kitchen. I called, "Hello, Lucy? It's me, Emily," and, from habit, opened the refrigerator. Inside was the familiar sight of leftovers saved in dishes with covers like little shower caps. "Hungry?" I asked Cliff. "I'm starved."

After dates, David and I would fool around here in the kitchen, and I'd start coffee, and then we'd sit at that old wooden table, I would sit on his lap, and we'd feed bread into the toaster. Hard-ons, and peanut butter toast.

Cliff said, "Didn't you get enough wedding cake?"

"I'm always hungry," I reminded him, and called again, "Lucy?" I went through the doorway, noticing that Lucy still kept a supply of elastic bands on the kitchen doorknob, something I myself did without thinking about it until one time I saw that Susan did also.

In the dining room now there was an overlay of Ma's possessions, and when we went into the living room the eyes of *The Laughing Cavalier* over the mantelpiece followed me eerily here as they had in Ma's living room. Bewildering, this blurring of things which belonged in Lexington with the things which had always been here, but in the midst of it all was Lucy's desk, as solid as the facts she corrected on it—spelling, arithmetic, the principal products of Holland—or as solid as the facts had seemed to me then.

I said, "That's Ned," and pointed to his picture on the console table. It had been taken when he was twenty; he wore a white shirt open at the throat and looked very Byronic.

I watched Cliff tour the room, examining baby pictures, childhood pictures, photographs of Lucy's classes in which the children were always young but Lucy, standing behind them as they sat with their hands folded primly on their desks, grew older in each, and when he stopped I thought he was looking at the snapshot John had taken after John and Susan's junior prom, Susan collapsed in a chair, legs outstretched under her gown, her junior prom queen crown of roses slipped down over one ear.

"Isn't that perfect?" I said. "Utter exhaustion—" and then I saw that he was looking at, instead, the snapshot Carol had taken of David and me outside the high school on a spring afternoon, David clowning, carrying my books. Granted, it was disconcerting that Lucy hadn't put away the picture, but why did Cliff seem so astonished? Oh, God, hadn't he realized Saundersborough was David's hometown, had he assumed we'd met in college? To fill the silence, I said, "There's Ma's wedding picture on the bookcase, and Lucy's," and as I crossed the room I saw that the wedding picture taken here in this living room after David and I were married was still on the mantelpiece beside John and Susan's. While I was staying here during the divorce, I'd supposed Lucy planned to put away such pictures discreetly, in time.

I called, "Lucy?"

"Emily?" Her voice came from upstairs. I went into the front hallway, which was the same as ever, furled umbrellas, walking sticks, the deacon's bench and telephone table dark under the stairway; but on the hall table was my great-great-grandfather's glove box that used to be on Ma's hall table.

Lucy rushed down the stairs. "Darling, how wonderful!"

We kissed, and I said, "Cliff brought me, Cliff Parker, the guy I wrote you I've been going out with."

She was wearing one of her summertime-vacation-time outfits, but her usually crisp blouse was limp with heat, and there were streaks of dust on her linen skirt. Her face was shiny with perspiration; her hands trembled.

"How wonderful," she said. "How wonderful."

As we went into the living room, Cliff turned from looking at the mantelpiece photographs.

She was startled by his beard, not so frequent a sight here as down around Hull. I hadn't thought to mention it, but I myself was startled that she showed her reaction. "Cliff," she said, and held out her hand, then noticed the dust on it and laughed shakily. This wasn't all caused by the beard. "We'd better not shake hands, had we? I'm covered with dust, but I'm so glad to meet you."

Cliff said, "And I'm very glad to meet you."

She said, "Kaykay's wedding was today, wasn't it? How did it go?"

"Just fine," I said.

"Have you been here long? I was up in the attic, then I thought I heard someone calling—"

I said, "This isn't exactly the sort of weather to be up in a hot attic, is it?"

"I wanted to get some things done—come, let's go out to the kitchen and find ourselves a cold drink, and I'll wash up." This reminded her; she was definitely rattled, or she would've mentioned it sooner, for, after years of children's bladders, she always immediately offered company the bathroom, mortifying Susan and me. She said, "Do you want to wash your hands, Cliff? The bathroom's upstairs."

"Thank you," he said, and went into the hallway while Lucy and I went out to the kitchen. She said, "There's some bitter lemon in the icebox."

Since when had she started drinking bitter lemon instead of tonic? "No, there isn't," I said. "I'll check the pantry, you probably forgot to put it in," and in the pantry there was a warm six-pack of bitter lemon sitting on the breadboard.

Lucy brushed at her skirt, her dusty hands making more streaks. "Well, with ice cubes, it'll be cold enough."

"You're just getting more dust all over you," I said. What the hell was the matter with her? "You'd better wash up first, then use the clothes brush." I went back into the pantry and found the clothes brush where it always was, dangerously mixed in the clutter of shoe brushes and shoe polish on a bottom shelf.

She dried her hands. "How long can you stay?"

"Oh, we'll have to leave soon." For where? I yanked the ice tray out of the refrigerator; it was a fiendish ice tray, and I slammed it around in the sink and turned on the hot water, the only way I'd ever been able to part it from its cubes. "How are things in town? What's new?"

"Carol's youngest boy fell out of a tree and broke his arm. He was building a tree house. Remember when you and Susan built a tree house out back?"

"Susan did most of the building. I decorated."

She said, "He seems a nice boy, Emily."

"I thought you said he was a classroom disruption."

"Not Carol's youngest. Cliff."

"Cliff. Yes, he is."

She removed her glasses, patted her face with a Kleenex, and took a little folder of glasses-cleaning tissues from where it always lay on the kitchen table near the pepper mill and the salt shaker which had rice added to its salt every summer to combat humidity. She tore off a tissue and rubbed her glasses. When I was little, I hadn't liked to see her do this, to see her face unfamiliar without her glasses, and even now I glanced away, but not before I saw how the violet wrinkles beneath her eyes sagged with tiredness. I was shocked.

I said, "Are you sure you should work at the summer session and take that course this summer? Why don't you have a real vacation for a change?"

She put on her glasses. "I'm going to."

"What? Well, that's marvelous."

"Emily, you know Mildred died four years ago. Sinclair's wife."

Sinclair Flanders was the lawyer who had married us. "Yes," I said. "Remember those Christmas cakes she used to make and give for presents, snowballs, that's what she called them, angel cake and whipped cream and lemon gelatin all mixed up and rolled in coconut—"

She said, very fast, "I planned to phone you, and phone Susan, tomorrow, and tell you now that it's settled. Sinclair and I are getting married July eleventh."

The gin bottle was Gilbey's, frosted, not smooth, so it didn't quite slip out of my grasp.

Cliff came into the kitchen. "There you are," he said.

I said, "Gin and bitter lemon?" and handed Lucy and him each a glass. "Excuse me, I'll be right back." I went out through the dining room and living room to the hallway and up the stairs.

The attic door was ajar. I climbed the attic stairs into hotness so intense it was almost visible. Sweat poured down me. Lucy had forgotten to turn off the attic light, something she would scold us for. I smelled mothballs.

When we used to play here, there was one trunk that was always locked. Lucy'd said she had lost the key. A big trunk, tantalizing, a mystery, though Lucy told us it contained only her old school books. It was open now, and in the cartons surrounding it on the dusty floor were its contents. Not school books.

Ned's clothes. I tried to remember noticing their disappearance from the closet in the big bedroom, but I couldn't. Everything else downstairs had remained the same—the pictures, his own books, boyhood books, school books, yearbooks, his skis and snowshoes and fishing gear and guns—all at first reminding, but then with the years becoming again part of the house.

Shirts, trousers, socks, underwear, pajamas. His fishing hat, the old floppy hat with flies still stuck in its sweatband. I picked up his canvas jacket and thought that very faintly through the smell of mothballs I could smell fly dope.

There were slow footsteps on the attic stairs.

I said, "Why did you stay in Saundersborough? You could have gone home to Lexington."

She said, "I could have gone anywhere, Emily. It wouldn't have made any difference where I was."

We stood in the suffocating heat. Then I put the jacket back in the carton, and she knelt to fold it more neatly.

She said, "But you and Susan. You were so young. I thought that leaving Saundersborough would truly kill him for you, and I didn't want that."

"This heat," I said. "Let's go downstairs."

She still fussed with the jacket. "I've never been on an airplane, I got thinking in case something happened I should clean out this trunk so you or Susan wouldn't have to do it."

"Airplane?"

"We're going to England and the Continent, three weeks of rushing around being tourists. We decided we might as well; it's now or never." She stood up.

I said, "I left Thornhill."

Practical, she said in her old matter-of-fact way, "You could hardly have stayed, could you? You wanted a job; did you want to take over the English position David vacated?"

"Lucy. You knew he was in Pleasantfield!"

"I met his mother once downtown, and she mentioned it. He's bought a house." She scrutinized me. "How did you know?"

"I met him by accident, this spring. Flying a kite at the beach."

"I see."

"He asked after you. He's bought a house?"

"Yes," she said. "He's not starting afresh, Emily. It's impossible. But he must have found it necessary to continue differently. Mercy, this heat!"

We went down the stairs, and she turned off the light and closed the door. She said, "You left Thornhill. Did it make any difference?"

"I've got to go in here, I'll be right down."

In the bathroom, I looked at my face in the mirror. My summer face. Freckles. I seemed to be breeding more and more freckles as I grew older. Living in North Riverton, I would find more freckles each summer when I looked in the mirrors at Cliff's farmhouse, freckles and summers, summers of gardens, as at Thornhill, summers of suppers on the porch, summers of hikes and fishing and picnics. It would all be the same as Thornhill, except for the house and a baby. Except for Cliff.

Out in the hall, I paused at the doorway of my bedroom, but I didn't go in. I could see my little desk, where long ago I had sat and written poems to David, poems with too many words like "silver" and "mist" and "bamboo."

Downstairs, Lucy and Cliff were sitting at the kitchen table, discussing remedial reading. The ice cubes in my glass on the sink counter had melted.

I asked, "Where will you live when you come home?"

"Here," she said. "Sinclair sold his house three years ago, and he bought one of those chalets in that new development, but he's pretty disappointed with it, in the winter it leaks from backed-up snow on the roof, and anyway, I refuse to live in a chalet. Holiday homes," she snorted.

I said, "Lucy's getting married, Cliff," trying to recall who Sinclair and Mildred's children were, a boy and girl much older than I.

"Just a small ceremony," she said. "We'd like you and Susan to come, if you don't mind seeing a couple of old fools—"

"Naturally, I'm coming," I said.

"What fine news," Cliff said to Lucy, but he was looking at me. "My best wishes." He raised his glass, and I sensed he was going to say something about our getting married.

His brown-and-gray curls, tousled from the swim; his blue eyes smiling. I could not make him into David. I must not try. He was not David. It would always be wrong because he was not David.

"No," I said to him. "No."

"What?" Lucy said, puzzled, and I quickly lifted my glass, but I couldn't think of a proper toast, so I said, "Happy days."

"Thank you, darling," she said. "Now, can't you stay for supper? I was going to have some consommé, and I believe there's some cheese—"

Cliff got up and put his glass in the sink.

Lucy said, "We could make Welsh rabbit, or is it too hot?"

I said, "We have to be starting back."

"Back to Hull?" Cliff said.

I said, "If you want to go on to North Riverton, I can get back somehow myself."

"There's no point in my going alone, is there? I can just as well telephone."

His voice was quiet, polite.

Lucy, watching us, said, "What are your plans for the summer, Emily? Are you going to write? If you want to stay here—"

"Thank you," I said, and used the first excuse that occurred to me, "but I've got summer school, I'm taking a couple more courses."

She beamed. "Are you really? Have you applied to graduate school so they'll count toward a master's? Let's see, you've got six credits already, and if you take two courses this summer and one each semester for—"

I kissed her. "But I'll be up July eleventh. What should I wear?"

"Oh, any summer dress. Maybe not so short as the one you're wearing? Cliff, it's good to have met you."

We went out to the car, and I remembered to look back and wave at her as we drove off.

Cliff's knuckles were white knobs. We drove in silence. My teeth were clenched so tight I couldn't have spoken. He didn't take any back roads, but drove directly south and got on the new turnpike east to Concord. Darkness came.

We were nearly back to Hull before he said, explosively, "Jesus Christ, Emily, Jesus Christ."

"I'm sorry," I said, I who knew that this was beyond apology.

We drove up the prism-colored Miracle Mile. It was frantic with traffic; the discount department stores were still open, their parking lots jammed with cars. The enormous Kentucky Fried Chicken bucket spun hypnotically, inviting us all to come in.

When he stopped the car in front of my building, we sat for a moment. He said, "Divorce is not death. Is it going to take you twenty years, like your mother?"

"I don't know."

He got out and gave me my suitcase and garment bag. I went indoors, hearing the car drive away.

Grace was watching television and eating a beet sandwich. "Hi," she said. "Everything went off well, didn't it? Even the flower girl—"

I stood and looked at the furniture which was not mine. Here I was.

I remembered how when Pop died, Ma left his room the way it had been, and in the living room his pipes still rested on the mantelpiece, and his armchair was still slick with their ashes.

I remembered our living room in Thornhill, the roll-top desk, the old sofa, the faded carpet, the walls of books.

I looked at the mock-traditional furniture, and everything seemed to stand out like those cut-out scenes I used to have when I was a kid; you unfolded them, and the trees and people popped up each alone against the background.

It didn't matter where I was.

I went into my bedroom and lifted the banjo out of the case. I began to play, listening to the clear high hiccup of the fifth string ringing.

• • •

The next day, after Grace had left for the car wash and her Sunday dinner, I went out to the Falcon. I'd studied the route to Pleasantfield so often I didn't have to get out the map to check it. I drove through scrubby woods, past the outskirts of poor towns. It was such dismal country; why had David come here?

While I drove I thought about how I had been when I first arrived in Hull and wondered what I'd be like now if I hadn't met Warren and Cliff.

At the sign for Pleasantfield, I turned off the road and drove along the main street. There were some houses which needed repainting, a dirty gas station, a general store with a beer and ale sign. And there was the school, a yellow clapboard building and a playground of empty swings and jungle gyms.

I drove back to the general store and sat, getting up courage to go in. When I did, I saw a telephone on the wall, and a phone book. Lewis, David E. The *E* meant Edward. 37 Warner Street.

"May I have a pack of Pall Malls, please?" I said to the man across the counter stacked with Sunday newspapers. "And could you tell me where Warner Street is?"

"First street on your left, young lady."

"Thank you. And the school down the road, is that the high school?"

"It used to be, but it's just the elementary school now."

"Where's the high school?"

"Out there on the main road. Keep on going half a mile, you can't miss it. It's one of them fancy ones. There's what they call the middle school, and there's the high school."

"Thank you."

I sat in the car and lit a cigarette. I would look at the high school first, and maybe that would be enough.

I drove on, and when I saw the sign BLUE POND REGIONAL, I knew immediately why David had come here. I parked in the driveway and looked at the spread of buildings, all brick and glass. I had heard of Blue Pond Regional. It was the sort of school you heard about, very experimental, so experimental for the towns it served that it was very controversial as well. An open-concept school, I remembered. Few walls, and the kids did a lot of sitting around on floors. Independent study. The teacher could decide whether or not his class should meet. The nucleus of the school was the library—no, not "library" but "learning center."

I looked at the school, trying to remember everything I'd heard. Here David came every day and was allowed to teach the way he wanted to teach and allowed to wear whatever he wanted to wear. How he used to hate having to wear a jacket and tie. I wondered what the teachers' room was like. A far cry from the boiler room at Thornhill, no doubt. Maybe it even was carpeted. Did Ann pack him a sandwich, as I had, or did he nowadays buy his lunch in the cafeteria? All the Spam sandwiches I'd made.

Seeing this wasn't enough, of course. I drove back to the main street and turned onto a street of old houses. I counted house numbers until ahead there were cars parked everywhere and I smelled hamburgers grilling on a barbecue. I parked where I was hidden by all the cars.

On the side lawn of an old cape, people were playing badminton, small children were playing croquet while a frenzied dog darted among them after the balls, and other people milled around drinking beer and eating hamburgers and hot dogs. David, beer in one hand, spatula in the other, presided at the grill. He was wearing a T-shirt and Bermudas. I'd never been able to talk him into buying Bermudas; he'd thought his legs looked ridiculous. There was Ann, more pregnant than ever, at the picnic table, spooning macaroni salad onto a paper plate for a little boy.

A party to celebrate the end of school. Teachers and their families, come one, come all.

I considered the cape, the motley patches of shingles where the roof had been mended at different times during the years, the paint flaking off the clapboards, and I saw that David had begun what would probably be his summer project, scraping and repainting.

He had always been so wary of buying a house. I remembered a party at the shop teacher's house in Thornhill; people were talking about buying homes, and David, drinking beer, was saying to an earnest social studies teacher, "Think of the upkeep. There'll be a leak in the attic or rot in the sills or rewiring for a clothes dryer, there'll be ten million things. Just ask me, I know all about it."

The social studies teacher said, "Not with a new house."

David said, "But there's fire you can worry about, and if you're a really good worrier like my folks you can rig up all kinds of alarm systems and gongs and more fire extinguishers than you've got furniture to extinguish, and there's lightning rods, too, and you must build a fallout shelter."

The social studies teacher began uncertainly to grin.

David said, "I come from a cautious family," and finished his beer. "My folks' cellar got flooded just once, but that was quite enough for my father; probably ours is the only house in the world with a bilge-level indicator in the cellar."

"Does it have a gong?" the social studies teacher asked.

"It has a gong," David said. "All they need now is a couple of antiaircraft guns on the roof."

Yet he had bought this house.

I looked at him. There were changes. But, still, he was I and I was he and there were all the years.

Ann walked over to him and took the beer out of his hand and drank. They stood together and watched the people at their party. David said something, and she laughed.

I turned the car in a driveway and drove back to Hull.

Readers' Guide for

One Minus One

Discussion Questions

1. What do you think happened to Emily after the end of this book? Did she "get over" David? Did she end up with Cliff?
2. What makes for a better life, following your heart or your head?
3. Why didn't MacDougall call the novel *Two Minus One*?
4. What would David's side of the story be?
5. How much sympathy did you have for Emily? What did you think about her behavior at the end of the book?

Suggestions for Further Reading

If you liked exploring the dichotomy between decisions made by the heart and those made by the head, and the difficulty of choosing which to follow, try these:

Esker, one of three main characters in Leah Hager Cohen's *Heart, You Bully, You Punk*, still believes she's in love with her college boyfriend nine years after he left her to marry someone else.

Barbara Gowdy's *The Romantic* asks this question: What do you do when you love someone who is hell-bent on destroying himself?

In Ann Packer's *The Dive from Clausen's Pier*, a young woman who suspects that she's fallen out of love with her fiancé has to decide whether or not to break the engagement after he has a life-altering accident.

The eponymous main character of Chaim Potok's *My Name Is Asher Lev* must choose between honoring his astounding artistic talent or remaining faithful to the tenets of his religion.

If you enjoyed the small-town New Hampshire setting of *One Minus One*, try these:

When outsider Naomi Roth discovers the body of a murdered child in the Sabbathday River, unraveling the mystery of who's responsible touches almost everyone living in the small town of Goddard in Jean Hanff Korelitz's *The Sabbathday River*.

Can you ever go home again (particularly where you were an intensely unhappy adolescent)? In *The Dearly Departed*, Elinor Lipman introduces us to Sunny, who comes home to King George after the death of her mother, Margaret, a woman beloved by the whole town.

Probably one of the truest pictures of coming of age in the 1950s, Ruth Doan MacDougall's *The Cheerleader* follows Henrietta Snow through her teen years as she navigates the intricacies of high school, friendship, and first love.

If you like to read novels about male/female relationships, try these:

How hard is it to rekindle an old romance? In *The Patron Saint of Unmarried Women*, Karl Ackerman humorously tells the story of Jack and Nina's on-again, off-again romance: once engaged, they're now both involved with other people.

In Barbara Pym's *No Fond Return of Love*, marked by Pym's trademark wry humor and affection for her main characters, Dulcie Mainwaring thinks she's found her true love—but can she persuade him that he feels the same?

As a child, outgoing Vaclav's great desire is to be a famous magician, and Lena, shy and reserved, becomes his trusted assistant and best friend. What happens when, through no fault of their own, they're separated? Haley Tanner's debut novel, *Vaclav & Lena*, sensitively limns this relationship.

About the Author

Photo credit © Tim Cameron

Ruth Doan MacDougall was born and grew up in Laconia, New Hampshire, where she started writing stories at the age of six—and never stopped. She attended Bennington College and graduated from Keene (NH) State College. After living for two years in England, she and her husband, Don, settled down in New Hampshire, where she writes novels, which include the national bestseller *The Cheerleader*. She also updates her late father's hiking books. On her Web site, www.ruthdoanmacdougall.com, she writes about life in the countryside.

She is a recipient of the New Hampshire Writers' Project's Lifetime Achievement Award.

About Nancy Pearl

Nancy Pearl is a librarian and life-long reader. She regularly comments on books on National Public Radio's *Morning Edition*. Her books include 2003's *Book Lust: Recommended Reading for Every Mood, Moment, and Reason*, 2005's *More Book Lust: 1,000 New Reading Recommendations for Every Mood, Moment, and Reason; Book Crush: For Kids and Teens: Recommended Reading for Every Mood, Moment, and Interest*, published in 2007, and 2010's *Book Lust To Go: Recommended Reading for Travelers, Vagabonds, and Dreamers*. Among her many awards and honors are the 2011 Librarian of the Year Award from *Library Journal*; the 2011 Lifetime Achievement Award from the Pacific Northwest Booksellers Association; the 2010 Margaret E. Monroe Award from the Reference and Users Services Association of the American Library Association; and the 2004 Women's National Book Association Award, given to "a living American woman who…has done meritorious work in the world of books beyond the duties or responsibilities of her profession or occupation."

About Book Lust Rediscoveries

Book Lust Rediscoveries is a series devoted to reprinting some of the best (and now out of print) novels originally published between 1960–2000. Each book is personally selected by Nancy Pearl and includes an introduction by her, as well as discussion questions for book groups and a list of recommended further reading.